SOMEWHERE
in
BETWEEN

SOMEWHERE
in
BETWEEN

LORA VANMETER

Ordering Information:

BookTrail Agency
8838 Sleepy Hollow Rd.
Kansas City, MO 64114

Printed in the United States of America

Somewhere In Between

It is a fact; the death of a single star outshines everything in its galaxy. A black hole forms a vortex of energy in its absence. What's left behind is ninety-nine percent invisible. Sometimes what we can not see makes us feel uncertain, but that doesn't mean we should stop believing in hope. The law of physics reminds us that everything we see in the universe is always from the past; believing in the present, we are already hoping for what's yet to come. A star's light can take decades to reach earth. When you look up into the night sky above, we are always reminded that somewhere a life has begun but ended.

The empty spot where my husband used to lay, revealed a dark invisible shadow where it seems someone is there; a phantom in the dark. Night after night I couldn't sleep, but the bad nightmares seemed so real. I pull away the cover's realizing that he is not in bed sleeping next to me. The morning sunlight is now peering through my curtains, I look down at the empty spot and realize that what I had worried about has come true…

It's tricky when your own story doesn't have a reliable author, but I knew what happened, it was my fault. We had gotten into an argument and I had distracted him from the road. I only suffered slight amnesia from a concussion on my head. My husband however, had been lying in a coma for two months, connected to the breathing machines. The foggy weather had been bad that night. We had been driving back home from celebrating his fifty-seventh birthday party. The other driver had not seen us in his blind spot, and had been killed. Not knowing why this happened, always made me question why God takes away what we love the most.

No one likes the feeling of guilt that makes you feel like you've done something wrong. It makes you feel powerless when you don't trust your own choices. We had waited two months. It was my choice to let them turn off the machines to donate my husband's organs. I wanted to believe that this could make a difference in someone else's life. I didn't want to let go; it was still the same fear that had haunted me from when I was abandoned and left by my mother as a baby. Like most of you, I held secrets under my scars. I had always felt incomplete because I had never known that unconditional love. However, I had learned that "terrible things can happen to you, but it's how you choose to handle it, that can make you stronger or destroy you."

Loving someone so much comes with a price; there's always' the fear of losing them. When the machines were finally turned off keeping my husband alive, it tore me apart. I felt abandoned, alone, and helpless, when no one else could understand. All those years that we had been married had slipped away so quickly when time had been our enemy. Consequently, I knew one thing, God would get me through if I trusted him with what would happen next in my life. I wanted to start over and go back to my hometown. I didn't forget my life I had left behind, but I wanted to believe in something greater.

Moving to the small city of Waynesville, Ohio I have decided to purchase an old empty Catholic church that has been turned into a furnished house. The old St Lindon's church had been where I was left as a baby. Due to fire damage long ago, I find out its past has a connection to mine. Wanting to resurrect it again gives me purpose as I go through my grief. It's funny how we all want to connect with something either it be a memory, an object, or a place that we still hold in our heart. I hadn't realized that my childhood neighbor whom had moved away when I was young, had taught me an important lesson about life. That sometimes a good book is best understood from the end to the beginning. Consequently, it's a scary feeling when you start to question your own purpose of what you must do to be happy in life.

Sometimes a good story should have a happy ending, but not all endings are meant to leave you feeling empty and lost. The stories about living and dying, they can help us face those obstacles that challenge us when we feel lost and alone. We can look at our universe and see the evidence that time is relative. It can teach us that this life isn't the only place where we will see our loved ones once again. It teaches us that grief and sorrow are just love persevering because everything is connected to something greater. This story is about the people who come into our lives, who show us how to believe in a universe that transcends beyond our own beliefs.

Chapter One
(Patty)

I can remember the moment precisely, that day they told me they were going to unplug my husband from the machines. It was the year 2011 on a warm spring day. I didn't know how to let my best friend go, when I thought he would stay with me forever. Only forty-nine years old I knew that loving someone isn't just a choice when you must trust that nothing bad will ever happen to them. The foggy weather and storm had been the cause of the severe car accident that night when we were heading back home on the highway. I had also blamed it on the argument we had. Distracted by his view Phillip did not see the large truck trying to merge in the lane before us. The roads had been foggy due to the rain. Phillip had loved that old grey Honda. As I watched the truck hit us, we suddenly slid, as it turned over onto the road. It was if time stood still as I watched before me in horror. It was April 11th and we were heading back from celebrating Phillip's fifty-seventh birthday at the bar and grill nearby only two miles away. I think about what we could have done; we should have gone a different way home. I wanted to remind Phillip that he could have taken the back road home but I didn't. I tightened the sweater around my chest and looked towards the busy road ahead. I looked at my watch. I thought everything was going to be okay.

We had lived in the town of Providence, Kentucky, a somewhat small town where I grew up in. However, I was born in 1962 in Waynesville, Ohio five and half hours away. Abandoned at birth, my mother left me hidden inside a Catholic church as an infant, until the priest had found me. I was taken to a nearby adoption agency, and stayed there for a while until the foster family was allowed to take me home. There had been some complications with terminating the open adoption. The other family had wanted to take away the parental rights of my mother because she was using drugs. Sadly, I was told that my mother had been missing for weeks until they found her body in a nearby lake. I wasn't told what had happened but the reports had suspected suicide. I had always wondered about my real mother and why she had left such a footnote in my life. I grew up forgetting about her but feeling incomplete as if I needed to find out the truth.

My adoptive family made sure I had a good home and was well taken care of. They told me to not worry about looking for more information about my mother because it would just upset me. I constantly questioned the matter. I had wanted to know who I came from and why I was abandoned. Had my mother been so crazy that she didn't want me? Or was she just trying to protect me by taking me to a church? I had tried my best to not question it as the years went by, but sometimes I wondered why I didn't go back to Waynesville sooner to look into her past.

It had only been two months since Philip had passed. I had money from the will so I left Providence, Kentucky to come back to Waynesville. When I saw that the old abandoned St Lindon church that I had been left at as a baby was up for sale, I couldn't refuse the offer. Waynesville was five and a half hours away and deciding to move from Kentucky was a big decision. The relator had told me the church had been up for sale since 1999 due to a tragic fire that happened seven years before. I had not remembered what had exactly happened. Most of the church was saved and remodeled over the years but the tragedy seemed to affect the whole town. For nineteen years the St Lindon's church stood empty because of the tragedy. I was given some old reports that described the dark shadows seen in the windows as if something was always haunting it. This had kept anyone from wanting to buy it or make it a home. Sadly, the church stood empty and abandoned. On the other hand, I didn't let it bother me.

I look around at my new place. The old church only had carpet in the basement the rest was all wooden floors. The first floor held a long corridor that followed into the sanctuary where the pew seats had been. It was mostly empty so I had used it to hang most of my large photographs and art on the walls. There was a fireplace towards the back and a cross still hung high on the wall above the alter. My bedroom was down the hall in a small prayer room. It was furnished with my large queen bed, my old white dresser, and Phillip's cherry wood bookshelves. I did not like the accordion style closets that held my clothes. Instead, there was an ugly brown plastic vile curtain that you pulled sideways to open and close them. The open plan and vaulted ceiling gave my church a comforting feel. My favorite area was the kitchen. The pipes gave a funny noise when I turned on the hot water. The old black gas stove stood in the corner of the room. It was rusted but big enough to cook enough food for an army. The pantry stood in the middle floor and the door would lock from the outside if I didn't keep it open. It was big enough to hold my kitchen table and a marbled island that had bar stools. The second floor downstairs had a wide carpeted floor basement where I kept most of my moving boxes. They had told me that the boarded -up-office in the far back, had once belonged to the priest Father Eugene. I thought it was strange that the door had been locked. I didn't like going down there because the only light on the wall was dim.

3

I look down at my hands, the charcoal pencil I held bled like a stain you couldn't wash away. I push up my bifocals. The picture I was trying to draw in front of me looked disfigured. It did not look like someone familiar. I wanted to remember the old photo of my mother from the newspapers. I did not have any other pictures of her. I was sure she had the same green eyes I had, dark hair, and small frame. Now that I was older, my hair had turned to salt and pepper as I wore it pulled back away from my face.

I had hit my head causing slight amnesia from the accident. I was trying to remember everything that I had forgotten. They told me that most things from my short -term memory would be harder to recall than my long-term memory. The priest Father Eugene who had been so dedicated to his church, had been the one who found me as a baby at this church door lying in a box. In a way, I am not sure why I never came back to meet him. The only story I had was the black and white newspaper clipping of that day in 1962. It showed a picture of me wrapped in a sweater lying in a box. I had been the mysterious baby that was abandoned by a mother who had possibly been on drugs and mysteriously jumped into a lake.

Even though I never knew the priest whom had taken me to the adoption agency, I didn't understand why I couldn't remember some parts of my life, when two months ago, I had been leaving the hospital without my husband wishing I could forget what happened. It didn't make it any easier, when I worried that leaving my home town would make me forget even more of my present life. However, I needed to go come back here so I could remember parts of my past, and dig up the secrets of my real mother.

The ghostly figure of my mother's features that emerged on my drawing pad started to look blurry as tears formed into my eyes. I somehow missed her in a strange way; even though I never knew her. How can you grieve over someone you never knew?

My drawing before me is of a girl running free through a field of daffodils. The picture mostly shows browns and blues, and the clouds are grey. The only color is the girls red sweater. The same sweater I had been wrapped up in so tightly as a baby when they found me. I wasn't sure what it had looked like because I had never seen it again after I was taken. My adoptive family would not give me much details about my mother. As the years passed, I grew complacent about it. Maybe I was afraid to face what had happened, or maybe I was afraid to find out that she never wanted me. I had pushed it off again and again of wanting to look for the newspapers about it. I had kept thinking my new life in Providence had made me forget, and I had buried my anxious questions into the back of my mind. I wanted to finish my painting as I put down my paintbrush but I couldn't. It felt like something was missing, maybe I just needed to give it time. However, I couldn't forgive what she had done. In my mind she always would be just a ghost that would always haunt my memory.

That foggy night it had been Phillips special birthday and we had wanted to go out and celebrate. I yelled at him because I had always worried about everything. We had been talking about his early retirement but he had wanted to work more hours. I had told him that I wanted him to spend more time at home. I was tired of spending late evenings alone I had told him. When Phillip was thrown towards my side from the impact, I did not realize that he had blocked me from hitting the windshield. Phillip hadn't known that his last words with me would be arguing over some stupid retirement plan. We had been so busy just trying to make everything perfect for his big day. We had just wanted to get home. I had thought the other car had seen us.

Growing up I had enjoyed reading books and when I had gotten older, I always buried herself in cheesy romance novels, hoping that the made- up characters would find a happy ever after. I had been so vain, always expecting that someone would come into my life and save me. I hadn't married yet and at thirty I felt old starting over and dating again. I had just been through a break up in a long- distance relationship. Five years had gone by until we realized it was too much. It was 1992 on a cold October evening when I almost gave up on everything.

Just weeks before I had been depressed after the break up. I had quit my job and my life seemed pointless. That night I had gotten too drunk from the local bar. I started questioning my purpose in life, and I kept wondering why bad things kept happening to me. Life didn't seem important anymore and I had felt so alone. My boyfriend had broken my heart and I had no one else to talk to. I don't remember why I was so upset it wasn't the first time I had lost a friend. However, it was if I had suddenly felt all alone again. I didn't think life was worth living anymore, so I stood on top of a nearby bridge two blocks from my apartment, and looked down at the waters below. I thought of all the people in my life who had loved me, but then I thought of my mother. It was very dark outside, as I turned around, I heard someone behind me. The strange man who had been walking by saw me crying and standing close to the edge, I recalled how silly I had felt. As I was about to step away, he yelled. "Hey, do you know what time it is?" Here was some stranger who had no idea who I was and had already wanted to connect.

"It's nine- forty-four." I had told him. I ignored him at first hoping he would go away, but like some angel, he reached out his hand as I took it and I stepped off the bridgeway. When he asked me my name as I stared at this stranger mesmerized by his dignity, I felt warm inside.

On my first date with Phillip the next day, it was late as we met at a Chocolate café just a couple blocks down the road from my apartment. I knew it was destiny the way he had found me.

He had been recently divorced but I didn't let that bother me. I remembered looking at his light brown hair mixed with grey, cut short on the top but long in the back eighties style. His eyes were the color of sandalwood, with one more hazel then the other. His face held a scruffy goatee that hid his crooked smile. Phillip was eight years older than me. I remember trying to understand this man whom I had just met hoping that he didn't think I was crazy.

When Phillip told me the story about the sudden loss of his oldest brother a year before I felt a connection. Someone had found the body, but the autopsy showed that it had been an aneurysm not suicide like they had thought. The good news was his brother had been an organ donor and helped save many lives. I opened up and told him about the story of how I was found abandoned like trash in front of an old church. It was as if I had been some secret no one wanted to face. When my mother was found dead in a lake, they couldn't really prove if it was an accident or suicide. I told him that I had questioned it every day. "I really was just getting over a bad breakup from month ago." I told him. "But I was just standing on the bridge looking down, I wasn't going to jump…"

"Where do you think we go when we die?" He had asked me. I had told him I was a believer in God and had hoped that good people went to Heaven and bad people went to Hell. He had also been raised in a Christian home by a father who was a pastor. We both had believed that God was in control of one's destiny. It seemed as if we both still carried that weight of sadness that a person faces when they lose a loved one due to uncertain circumstances. "Do you want to go for a walk?" I had asked him.

It was dark outside in the fifty-degree cold as we strolled down the road along the streetlights that evening. It was my idea; I didn't want that first date to end yet. That evening had been so perfect, and yet I never felt this way with anyone else before. I wasn't ready to trust anyone yet but there I was pouring out my soul to this stranger. We both felt some connection as if fate had put us together, as if we had always been long lost friends. He questioned me how we barely knew each other and why I trusted him along the dark sidewalk away from the streetlights? I had forgotten my gloves and I had mentioned that my hands were cold. But when he took me by the hand, I reached for something that seemed so familiar like a memory from my past... I felt love and deep down I knew that I had found someone who understood what it was. As I looked up into the empty starless sky I didn't know if I would ever see him again after that night.

However, this time maybe in a way, I didn't want to let myself carry that hope of falling in love again just yet. But as he got into his car, Phillip looked back at me and said, "I will call you tomorrow Patty." I hadn't realized that after being married to him eighteen years later, "tomorrow" had been the only word I had held onto for so long. When I had faced day after day without him, wondering how I could have saved him I thought about what he had meant. "Sometimes that's all we need to believe in to move on." He had told me. "The sun will go down, but 'tomorrow' it's not that far off." I hadn't realized that was all I had ever wished for. I needed someone to direct me so I would be reminded of the hope that life can give. Phillip had been the only life line I had relied on, now it was my turn to save myself.

After we were married, I began to have strange dreams. It was the same nightmare every time. Something is wrong, and I can't breathe or hear. There is a bright light shining in my eyes. When I look down, I realize I am floating high above the ceiling. Someone is in the bed in the room connected to lots of machines. I can't see who it is underneath the blankets but whoever it is I feel connected to them as if I am waiting for them to wake up.

When I awake from the dream, the front of my night shirt is wet, the sheets are damp under me, and my heart is beating so fast. My head hurts as I lie back down again, I didn't understand it. But as I look over at Phillip's still body lying so peacefully next to me under the blankets, I close my eyes and go back into my lucid dream. Soon I am awakened by the light coming from the windows and my bed is empty again.

I had a full- time job at a nursing home as an art therapist for nineteen years. I had gotten the job a month after me and Phillip were married. I loved helping the seniors learn to handle a paint brush and paint. We had already discussed that we didn't want children. The reality was even though I longed to know what it was like; I didn't want to carry that burden of being a mother. My real mother had left psychological scars on my heart. She had left an empty space in my life. However, my adoptive parents had been the best role models I could ever have. It was okay that we didn't want children but sometimes I had wondered what it might have been like.

I felt loved so much by my husband that I didn't want to think otherwise. On the other hand, in the back of my mind, I thought of my own childhood I had missed. I had a next-door neighbor whom I had grown up with in Providence, whom had moved here to Waynesville a long time ago. We hadn't kept in contact over the years until I had gotten the invitation to his wedding. The last time I saw Luke, I had been eleven and he was thirteen. In the last letter I received from him he told me that he was doing great and had found the love of his life. The return address had Waynesville; Ohio posted on it. I didn't go to his wedding because I had been away in art school at that time. Now at forty-nine and him two years older, I wondered if he and his wife still lived at the same address.

Luke had been born with atrial septal defect or a hole in the heart. I had brushed it off as something not serious but his mother had told me that he wouldn't live pass fifty unless there was a donor. More than anything, I made sure that she would contact me if anything had happened. He on the other hand didn't seem to care, he had thought he was invincible. I had always believed that we would be besties forever. When I didn't hear back from him over the years I didn't think otherwise. But I learned the hard way; I should have kept in touch.

Chapter Two
(Patty)

I remember the day Phillip and I decided on a pet. We didn't have a fenced in area at our apartment so we decided to get a cat. I had just turned forty and wanted something to take care of outside of working. Blue was a big black cat we had rescued from a special pet adoptive center. He was just two years old and thirteen pounds when we met him. The funny thing was he had chosen Phillip that day when we walked into the nursery. When the attendant opened the door, the cat came right up to us and followed us around, while all the other cats choose to ignore us. When we found out that his birthday was the same as our anniversary, we saw that as a sign and that he was meant to be ours. The only problem was he had a respiratory illness that needed care and expensive medicine. No one else had wanted the common black cat with the heavy breathing that gave him the nickname of Darth Vader. However, when we took him home, his name became Blue and he was very lovable. I had thought like most, that black cats were mean or unpredictable. But this cat was special even though he had this uncurable sickness. He wanted attention and even loved to be held, scratched, and pampered. It was as if that ugliness everyone had labeled onto him, had caused him to suffer, adding to his sickness, as if marking him under some kind of curse.

In the same way, I knew what that cat felt like, to not be accepted for your flaws, to be stuck under a label as if you are not good enough. Being left with an adoptive agency, I learned at a young age to never feel unconditional love from anyone at first. Why pretend to want to be wanted when someone will always hurt you in some way? When we crawled into bed at night Blue would move at the bottom of the bed and sit his thirteen pounds on top my feet as if pining me down. In the mornings he would look up over the covers at us, as if wanting to make sure we were still there. If you were sitting down in a chair, he wouldn't just sit in your lap but he had to climb onto your chest so he could feel your warmth and be near your heartbeat. Yes, I knew what it felt like to wonder who would love me, who wouldn't push me away, or who would never give up on me no matter what.

As I thought about Phillip, I always wondered if we had planned enough ahead of time in case something terrible happened to one of us. I never imagined I would have to play God and decide his fate for him. I was always careful about every choice I made because when you run out of options your choices become more desperate. When you marry someone, it is for sickness and death. I had chosen him, and I had vowed to never stop loving him despite whatever happened. But how do you make that choice for them when they can't? How do you know when to give in?

I didn't really know why I wanted to work at a nursing home, maybe, because I liked to be around death; reminding me of what I had kept. Those old people were stuck in a prison; they had loved someone they had lost too. Like me, they held memories they could choose to remember. But sometimes when you choose to forget those you miss, you build this wall around what you want to remember. The filmy grey layer of denial comes off and you realize you have never let yourself feel that hope that still carries your broken heart. You want it gone because you feel you don't deserve it.

One day a nice elderly woman began to befriend me. She was in her eighties and after my shift she wanted me to listen and talk to her. I had told her I was a Christian and she also was a strong believer in God being brought up in the Catholic church. She seemed moody at times until day by day her layers began to unravel, as she told me about her husband that she lost. She had lost her sixty-four-year-old husband due to a young drunk driver's mistake. I felt something inside me want to listen as she cried. She had been in the car, and she had seen her husband die instantly. To make matters worse she had to deal with her attorney and the court over the accusations of the sixteen-year-old on her own. He had only gotten ten years in prison, but she had to forgive the person who took her husband and her life away. She needed someone to hear her story of how she had persevered among the worst of circumstances. When she told me how hard it was to forget that day, I couldn't imagine what I would do in her situation. She had lost her home, her finances, and her hope. Fighting over money and court rights she had lost trust in the only family she had left. Now with just a suitcase of memories to call her own, she told me how she had felt alone with nowhere else to go. "God, is the only friend who can get you through anything, but I will always blame myself for letting it destroy me." She had told me.

As I tried to understand her circumstances there was something in her eyes that made me feel like she already knew something about me. It was like she was an image of hope looking back but forwards into the future; a premonition of something to come. She had lost someone she had loved due to an accident, and she had to live with that grief forever. She had to learn to rely on God so she could someday move on. Now that she was on her own, something inside her had grown stronger. She had told me, "There are two ways to live your life, as if life is happening for you, or as if life is happening to you…"

I don't remember much from when I was left at that adoption agency so long ago but I remembered being held for the first time by my new mom. I didn't trust anyone then, but I also remember not wanting to let go of whoever tried to hold onto me. In the same way, I knew what it felt like to have to start over and learn to trust someone all over again. When my adoptive mother held me for the first time despite my angry cries, I remember that she was crying too. Even though she was a stranger to me she held me close to show me that she would never let me go. She wanted to show me that unconditional love meant never giving up, even when the situation is not what you expected.

Maybe what I had learned was that life doesn't always give us what we want. Because when you really have to surrender to whatever happens and when everything you had trusted in is left exposed, you realize that you are the only one who can untie the knot. There will always be conflicts we must face. No matter how much power it has over you sometimes you have no other choice then to find within yourself that shelter. When the path ahead doesn't look safe, all you can do is not look back at the things that make you feel insecure. At this point in my life, I felt hopeless. I kept flying into those ambient clouds trying so hard to find my way around the storm. I couldn't trust myself to look ahead. However, sometimes no matter how dark the clouds seem, the only way to save yourself is to not fly above the storm but right into it.

I don't remember much of what happened on that foggy unpredictable April night. I knew that Phillip had been looking forward to his birthday and sharing the red velvet two- layer cake I had made. The terrible thing was, if we had turned around to take the back roads instead maybe it never would have happened. However, I knew that there had always been something lurking outside of my security, waiting to come out and overtake me on that narrow bridge that I thought was strong. When I had been at the darkest point in my life, I wasn't able to look ahead. I couldn't get those sad songs out of my mind, they always reminded me of someone's past. What was it they were always' singing about? Death? Or Heartbreak? I had grown up hearing those lyrics of, "I'll be gone…" by David Bowie as if it was reminding me of what I had lost and what I was afraid of. Whatever it was I couldn't get the thoughts out of my mind. The fact was I knew there was something greater above the dark tragedies of this world. I wanted to believe in something I couldn't see. It was the doubt that weakened me and made my suffering worse.

Chapter Three
(Patty)

I remember as a child, in our old neighborhood of Providence, there was an old railroad track that my dad had passed over every day. We had to go that way in order for me it to get to and from school. I didn't like waiting for that train to pass, hoping it would come soon so we could get to the destination. My dad would even tease me about why waiting was so important. I asked my dad why we couldn't go a different way around it or turn around. But he explained to me that the roads didn't have a back way towards home. He explained that obstacles in life, like that train would pass, we just have to be patient and wait. Sometimes, we should face that detour in front of us, even if it blocks the direction we want to go. I hadn't realized it then, but my father had taught me such an important lesson in life. I couldn't see from where we were parked, how long that train had to get to the end, and I didn't know how long we had to wait. My dad had gripped the steering wheel so hard I could see the whites in the knuckles of his hand. He was trying to be patient too. He explained to me "Honey, sometimes you must let go of your expectations of where you want to be, because most of life is living in between, waiting for what you want."

As day's passed, I would wake up feeling hopeful that the day would end of Phillips coma. I would feel just a touch of hope as I had planned it out. There would be no obstacles in my way to keep me from believing for a miracle. By the time I had arrived at the hospital, gotten a nurse and into his room Phillip would be sitting up awake, and confused as I would tell him everything; how much I had missed him, how much I had needed him, and then we would go home. I had believed he would open his eyes just for me. I had hoped he would hold on a little longer just for me. I couldn't reach him, I couldn't help him find his way, and I didn't want to admit that I wanted to give up too. Like waiting for that train, I didn't want to stay still because I wanted to move ahead and find a better way around this. Would waiting another month have given him just enough time to finally wake up? or would he still be laying their leaving us anticipating? I was reminded of an important bible verse. It was about waiting on God instead of trusting in our own understanding. Psalm 37:7; "Be still and rest in the Lord; wait for Him and patiently lean yourself upon Him; fret not yourself because of him who prospers in his ways."

When I was a little girl, I told my parents I wanted a pet bird, and even though I wasn't sure how to care for it, I was sure I could. I had needed to make sure I covered its cage at night so it wouldn't get cold. I had to take it out daily so it could get used to me, and I had to make sure it's always' had plenty of food and water. However, when we left for a week to visit my grandparents across town, a bad winter storm had thrown the electricity out of our house for several days. We had not known if our house had been affected until we got home. My father had said the cage was covered and if the bird got cold, it would be okay. I didn't even sleep a wink as I worried all night, afraid of what I might face when we got home. I wanted to believe that somehow that bird was strong enough on its own. I wanted to believe that the bird would wait for us to come home. However, when we arrived back home days later to a cold house, I lifted the heavy blanket off and underneath I saw that the poor bird had died as it still stood on its perch. Its eyes were still open as if it had wanted to look straight ahead waiting for us to turn on the heat. But we had been too late the bird had given up on waiting. Maybe, it had known all along that someone would rescue it. Maybe it had relied on us too much not knowing the cold bitter sting of suffering. The blanket hadn't been enough to save it, its food wasn't enough, and the comfort of its home. Its security taken; all it saw around it was darkness. The bird wasn't strong enough to survive, but we thought it could wait protecting it from the coldness. Did the bird die because it hadn't learned to be strong? Or had the bird already decided to give up because it couldn't see what lay outside its door?

With Phillips coma, I wished that I could find an answer to why God makes us wait. I felt like I was behind some wall not knowing what lie ahead where I had to listen and be still in the moment. Likewise, waiting is not passive, it is a commitment. I didn't want to feel like that stupid bird left to endure the cold reality of trusting in something outside my comfort to rescue me. I felt like God was testing us to see how patient I could wait. Did this mean I didn't love my husband enough if I gave in and moved ahead? I was so tired of thinking of myself when I needed to think of what was best for him, not me. The truth was we had to learn that God was in control of this not us. The doctors told me if he awoke from the coma the damage to his brain would likely cause amnesia, loss of coordination, years of rehabilitation, and he would be relying on the hospital for the rest of his life. He probably wouldn't remember me. All the good memories that we had shared would be erased from his mind forever. The doctors had told me he had a thirty percent chance of recovery. How sad I thought, to have to start all over again. Could I live with that? and pretend that he would come around? Could he fall in love with me again?

When I looked into his face one last time, I was sure I heard him secretly whisper to me in my mind, "Please let me go..." I looked at the life support machines that he was hooked up to, he looked so vulnerable yet strong. I touched his now grown beard turning ash grey, and the small grey mustache above his soft lips. When the doctor came in to check on him, I told them we were ready to sign the papers. Phillip's organs would be donated to those who were waiting. My voice was nothing but a whisper. "God please comfort those who are waiting." I didn't want to hear myself say it, but it was too real.

It had been two months and there were people who needed organs. When I thought of them taking pieces of my husband and tearing him apart, it broke me. Who were these people who needed organs? What would it matter if we saved another life? As I sat in the hospital waiting room I couldn't stop worrying. Had I made the right choice? but as I looked at the list of families still waiting for doners, I knew what we were supposed to do. Maybe this was all meant to happen, maybe I was meant to be there at that moment signing over those papers, and maybe he was meant to give a life to save another. Phillip had always been my angel, he had been the one whom I thought saved me, but this time it was my turn to save a part of him. His purpose was to help those who were waiting to live.

Chapter Four
(Patty)

I look around at the St Lindon Catholic church that is now my home. The creaky wooden floorboards still gave way underneath when I walked on them. The smoke stains on the ceiling still marked the fire, the uneven window panels that wouldn't open all the way, and shadows that danced through the stained-glass windows were reminders of what was lost. The only part of this church I did not like was the basement. It was the only part of the place that seemed forgotten. I had to store some boxes down there when I moved in but I had never liked going down into basements.

Basements are dark places you leave alone, a place where you can lock up all the things you don't want to remember or find. It's good on its own where it can hold dust, dirt, cobwebs, smells and empty space. No one likes them because they might expose or reveal what you have lost. It could be a spider hiding in the corner, a dead mouse lying under the furnace, or a lost photograph you don't want to find. We don't like the thought of something hiding and unknown exposed and left for us to question. So, we abandon it. We pretend that what we don't see is not there. Because if we come across something that threatens our safety; we might not like it. Are we willing to accept its flaws, its mistakes, or its vulnerability? We don't like the thought of trying to let go of something that we once held close.

This church I had owned now was special because it was resilient. I wasn't sure why this town didn't want to remember what had happened and why it had been empty for so long. When I packed my bags and left Providence behind, I knew I wasn't making a mistake when all along I knew I was making the right choice. It had been waiting for me to come back to it all along, as if waiting for someone to accept its infirmity. I had felt some kind of connection to it as I looked around and unpacked my boxes. I hoped it would get my mind off the grief I was going through.

I think of yet another date Phillip and I had been on. I had remembered mostly details. I knew I was the first to tell him that I had loved him. I wasn't sure at first how he felt or would react. We were only seeing each other once a week around our schedules. Phillip would pick me up and then drop me off at my apartment. No kisses or hugs were exchanged yet but he would come inside later and talk as we sat together on my sofa. When I told him how I felt he reached for my hand, he didn't need to speak words, but the connection was louder than any expression. I knew we had been waiting a long time to finally kiss. It felt so relieved to find someone whom I trusted and had felt the same. It's a powerful feeling when you're in love. However, love isn't just a feeling it's a choice. You choose to become vulnerable exposing every flaw and insecurity and you choose to accept theirs too. In a way, the only way to truly fall in love is to not hold on so tightly to those things that you want to control. You need to give yourself room to breathe so you can know when the time is right. This time I truly felt happy as if it had been waiting for me all along. "Where have you been all my life?" we had asked each other.

However, there's nothing in life that can prepare you either for losing that person. You feel like the whole world has ended and that nothing else matters. You stay in your own little bubble thinking that no one understands. But the reality is people face it every day. Just turn on the news and someone has died somewhere in the world. I knew it would take time for the euphoria feelings I had relied on to wear off after Phillip had died. I was constantly reminded of an old eighty's song sung by Cindy Lauper. "Time after Time."

"After my picture fades and darkness has turned to grey, watching through windows you're wondering if I'm okay. If your lost you can look and you will find me, Time after Time. I've got a suitcase of memories that I almost left behind…"

It was what I had regretted the most. Time had been our enemy. All those years before, I had held back not letting anyone know me for who I was. Therefore, I didn't think I was worthy, full of doubts, flaws, and insecurities letting my past define me. I hadn't taken any chance at real love beforehand. Only letting those close to me get so far until the relationship would die. Consequently, growing older made me wiser. I had learned to find someone who loved me unconditionally for who I was. There is no deeper feeling than relying on failed expectations. It scares you when you are not in control of your own universe. It was something I had felt as a child when my neighbor Luke had moved away. The only way I could change was to stop looking at the past. I had grown tired of looking in my mailbox waiting for those letters we had promised to write. As time went on, I grew sorrowful, wondering if it was too late. When I left my small town in Kentucky to go to art school in Minneapolis the house next door was still up for sale. I didn't look back in despair at the empty yard me and Luke had played in. This time I had a new horizon to explore. In the same way, I didn't look back in regret in wondering how I would survive as a widow. They say you can't forget negative moments but positive moments can fade with time. I liked believing that my future ahead was clear but I didn't like the uncertainty. All along I had learned that hope had been my weakness.

֍

Chapter Five
(David)

Some people were scared of the woods at night, but not David he liked the dark shadows that played on the trees, it was the only place that made him feel safe and secure, like a blanket on a cold night. He had grown to love the small town of Waynesville since a young boy when they had moved from Louisville. The simple white churches, the small police office down the street, and the old cozy restaurants that lined the streets were things he had grown used to. The antique shops lining the sidewalks with their dozens of forgotten objects; each carried a story of its own. He was rooted to this town by his name and the slowness and laid- back atmosphere of the town. It had been the only thing he had known.

David had wanted to understand it, the meaning of life and one's purpose. He had grown up under the Catholic upbringing of his mother. She had been devout wanting him to follow in its teachings. They had been attending the St Lindon's Catholic church for years until the tragic fire had shut it down. As a young man he had become interested in the faith. When he had gotten older, he went to seminary school in Louisville and returned to his hometown of Waynesville, Ohio to become a priest at St Mary's. He wanted to help people because he enjoyed making the world a better place for everyone. David was an average looking man. Tall in stature, it was the only good feature he had, along with his greyed hair making him look wiser. Now at sixty-seven over the years he had become weak, powerless, and more damaged from the inside foundation of the faith he had built his life upon. The circumstances around him, the terrible things that went on in the world, and the freedom he once felt made him sarcastic towards the hopefulness he should be standing for. David held his secrets tight, but just like the rest of the town it seemed he couldn't get away from the anxiety. It had shed into his conscience always reminding him of how delicate life could be.

Six months ago, David had found out he had lung cancer. It was too late to save his right lung and he had been on the waiting list for four months for a new doner. The whole church had been praying for him. Until they had found a match, he hoped he would be given a second chance. Undergoing the major operation just six weeks ago had been difficult. He had been lucky they had caught the mass or he wouldn't have recovered. He didn't think something like this would ever happen to him. He wasn't ready to die yet, it made him think of so many things he still needed to do with his life. He was older now but there was something from his past that he still needed to face.

In time he stopped watching the news, he stopped praying for the hungry and he stopped donating to the nearby food bank. He knew that anger can only consume you when you let it; it can grow from the inside out, taking up space leaving its roots behind, growing further down cutting off every vein leading to malnourishment. He was angry at himself for not accepting that what was happening in the world was the result of man's sin. He wished that he could help people understand that they didn't have to carry their burdens alone. He didn't know what to do when he sometimes passed a homeless person holding up a sign that said, "Please help, need money." He never knew if they were on drugs or if they were being truthful. He did his best trying to survive in the world, reading his Bible daily, and trying to get through his struggles.

When he and his mother Sarah had first started going to the St Lindon's Catholic church, he remembered looking into the cold blue eyes of Father Eugene. The man had stood strong on his podium and taught them about the Catholic faith. Likewise, he had also scared him telling them that God was always watching, and to be on the look -out for temptation lurking around the corner. He watched as his mother carried her rosary everywhere and did the sign of the cross. He grew content with the security of finding a greater purpose, but he didn't like all the rules and the guilt that came with it. David had always believed in a God who loved him, but he couldn't understand the meaning of death.

When his father had died in the war, he had become confused about it. He was just a boy, but he had wondered; Was there really a place called Heaven and Hell? He remembered the day that Father Eugene had given him the book by Swedesboro called "Heaven and Hell." He had become fascinated by it trying to understand the meaning of one's purpose. Was death parallel to birth? What was God's purpose of death? These were questions that perplexed his frame of mind as a young man.

In 1962 David had lost the love of his life at eighteen to a terrible tragedy. His friend Mary was found in the lake weeks later under a bridge where no evidence could prove if it was an accident or suicide. Mary had attended St Lindon's church where he had met her in Sunday school class every week. She was so pretty with her long dark hair and green eyes. She hadn't grown up in a safe environment, losing her parents at a young age. She had been moved around from different foster families. He had enjoyed getting to know her as they had grown so close. They had to secretly meet in the back woods because she was closely watched by her foster family. David had heard that she had been doing drugs before and was kept under strict rules. When it had gotten worse, he wanted to save her from the addiction she had tried to break.

One day when she told him she was pregnant he knew he was the father. He remembered how angry and scared she had been when he told her not to have an abortion. They had agreed to not tell anyone outside the family that she was carrying his child. It was a small town and sooner or later she would be questioned. Mary agreed to go away during those nine months to stay with Sarah, David's mother, as she was home schooled. She promised to give the baby up for adoption, to a family that would be waiting, when the child arrived. Father Eugene, Mary's foster parents, and his mother were the only ones who knew she was pregnant. David had been accepted to go into seminary school that year after he graduated, however, he did not want this to affect his life either. In a way, he hoped the baby would be adopted by a family close by, but instead, the family who had wanted the child, lived five hours away in Providence, Kentucky. Mary had wanted it to be an open adoption but she was required to take care of her drug problems first.

David remembered that day when his mother had called him. Mary had the baby girl in the neighbor's barn, she did not make it to the hospital. There were complications. His mother Sarah had been there during the birth. When she left Mary alone for a moment and came back Mary and the baby were gone. They had not known that she was going to run away with the baby. "Where is she?" David had asked his mother when he arrived at the house. "I think she took the baby and ran away with it, she said she changed her mind." Mary already had signed an agreement for an adoptive family but instead she hadn't realized the mistake she had made. The police were contacted to search for the mother and baby. "It's too late," his mother told him. "The child belongs to someone else and we need to find them before she gets arrested."

Sarah hadn't realized that Mary was desperate when Father Eugene had called her. He had found a missing baby lying in a box inside the church door. Father Eugene was greatly surprised when she told him Mary and her baby had been missing. Inside with the baby was a letter signed by an anonymous person. "Please take my child and baptize her, protect her from the tragedies of this world." It had said. It soon was reported over the news and the whole town had questioned who and where the mother was. However, Father Eugene pretended he did not know anything about it.

David thought she was his child, but he had no other evidence but to take her to the hospital to reveal the identity. The family had wanted to press charges when Mary disappeared. When the baby was taken to the hospital, the DNA revealed that the child was David's. "Why would she do this?" his mother had asked him. When David heard that his baby was taken to social services to be taken home by the family from Providence, his heart sank. He had wanted the adoption to stay open so he could visit secretly someday. Mary was still missing, and he assumed she was somewhere homeless and using again. Had she decided on doing drugs again and given up? He had wanted his mother to support him as they prayed and hoped that Mary would return.

When a week passed, they grew worried. David had thought that Mary would come back. Two days before, he had received a phone call from her. "I am going to leave Waynesville. I can't do this anymore. I am going to put my life back together. Please keep my baby safe. I can't tell you where I'm going." she had told him." "Goodbye, I love you." David had worried because she had no money and would be by herself. He hadn't known where she was going but he hoped she meant that she was going to do the rehab required for her drug problems.

When Mary's foster family had questioned him, David had no answers. He had been questioned by Father Eugene that if he knew anything to give details to the police. However, he had wanted to protect her. He hoped that she was okay and would follow the requirements of the adoption. He had warned her to be careful. "It's not an open adoption anymore you can't just interfere." He had warned her. "I know I messed things up, but I just want to hold her again someday." She had argued with him, "Then you must obey the law and do rehab first." David had told her. He was hoping that afterwards she would just let it go.

That night when he was leaving the St Lindon's church, he had been up late writing his seminary essay for his acceptance application. David heard someone come into the back door. When he walked back up the stairs after closing up Father Eugene's office to see who it was, he noticed the new candles burning on the alter. It was dark in the sanctuary. "Who's there?" he asked. As he slowly walked towards the pews, he felt afraid even though he was in a church. Sometimes homeless people would come by during the day to sit inside to pray but never at night. As he looked closer, he saw someone sitting in the front pew. "Mary is everything all right?" he recognized her shadow and the same sweater she always wore.

"Because of the drugs, I never will be good enough to be a mother. Will I? I messed up again and now I won't be able to see her? But I'm trying so hard, why can't they give me a second chance?" David tried to emphasize with her.

"Mary, please, we can help you, but the family wants to press charges, and this doesn't look good on your record. You need to turn yourself in and do rehab it's the only way to get their confidence back. I'm sorry." When David stood up, Mary suddenly took her bag and ran towards the door. "It's not fair that I could have had something of my own to love, and now it has been taken from me. I'm going to the train station." She seemed upset and he wasn't sure if she had been using again. "You are just making it worse by running away..." he yelled after her. Mary had already gone out the door down the road, it was late and David needed to get home. He watched as she disappeared into the dark night. He had thought she would want to listen, but the police were looking for her. He kept thinking that he should have followed her down the street. He should have told her that he still loved her no matter what mistakes she had made. He hadn't known it was the last time he would ever see her again.

The next morning his mother Sarah had told David that she found a copy of a train ticket in Mary's room. She had accused him of helping her, asking him if he had seen her, or given her money. He had told her that Mary had come to him about wanting to leave town but she had seemed upset over the charges against her. He did not know what to do, but he didn't run after her or call the police after they had spoken. When his mother showed him the rosary, she said she had found on the bridge, he worried something had happened to her. No one had seen her for over twenty-four hours. "We must report it to the police." He told her.

David still had Mary's rosary in his drawler. It was always in the shelve by his bedside. The police had questioned them afterwards but he could tell that something wasn't right. When the body was retrieved from the lake a week later, he couldn't deny the fact that his mother was hiding something from him. He had held onto that rosary as if he thought it would somehow redeem them from the lies. He knew his mother had seen Mary that night after Mary had come to him. His mother had said something to upset her. In a way, he didn't know why he had been so angry about it. His mother had just wanted to help her so she could get the legal rights to see her child someday. He had always felt that if he had known that his mother was going to interfere, he would have stopped it. He felt they both were to blame for Mary's death and that's why he kept his mouth shut.

᪐

Chapter Six
(Patty)

I open my eyes and look at the clock. Four-twenty-four am, it reads, as if shouting at me with bright red numbers. I couldn't sleep, it was a full moon outside and the brightness shone through my window. I take a deep breath and listen to the faint knock coming from my basement. I sit up but the noise wouldn't go away. Since I had moved in every night at the same time I was awakened by the same noise. I get up and throw my robe on. I open my bedroom door. I can hear the faint thudding of my own heartbeat in my ears. In the silence it starts again, the tapping sound was coming from underneath down there, I could hear it from my room. It was just above the stairs from the basement. It was coming from that boarded- up office room that had belonged to the priest. Why they hadn't cleaned it out upset me. It was like they didn't want to mess with it.

I kneel down onto my floor and listen again. "TAP, TAP, TAP", sometimes it would get louder. I stand up curious, but I do not want to go down there at night. It made me feel creepy as the hair on my neck felt static every time. Maybe I should have someone check for racoons, I think. I try to rationalize what it could be. I knew my hot water heater was broken, but I didn't think something like that would make that much noise. Old places like this could have all kinds of strange creeks as the wind outside shuffled the frame.

As a little girl my first memory was of our beautiful new yellow house we had just moved into. It was 1969 and I had loved it because I had my own room with yellow carpet, a big closet, bunk beds with rainbow sheets and aqua blue paint on my walls. Posters of unicorns decorated my walls and I had a toy box full of stuff animals. My parents did not let me have any pets because my dad was allergic. They thought I was happy with all my toys and dolls but the reality was I had wanted something else real that I could talk to. I grew lonely and started developing my own imaginary animal friends. My parents thought I just had an extraordinary imagination.

One day a boy named Luke moved into the house next door to us. When I went over that day to meet him, I told my parents that I had just met Luke who was eight and close to my age. Even though my mother didn't believe me at first, she pretended to listen. Luke had light auburn hair under his sad brown eyes. However, he had a strange mark on his face. When I described his strange two- inch red birthmark that covered the left side of his cheek and how it ran all the way down to his chin, shaped like a crescent moon, my mother stared at me wide eyed. Maybe he isn't real she had told me.

When Luke came over one day with his mother to visit us, my mother nearly fainted realizing they were the new neighbors next door. I was told that Luke had something wrong with his heart. His mother became good friends with my mother and I was told to be gentle with him when we played. Over the months me and my friend spent a lot of time together as if we were meant to be. I didn't care if kids at school made fun of him but I worried when he got his feelings hurt. He might have been different but he wasn't ignorant of his flaws. When the bullies in our neighborhood saw us, I wanted to protect him from the awful world that couldn't see him for who he really was. Even though we did not see each other at school because of our grade differences, I made sure to go over and play with him in the evenings to keep him company. Luke was shy at first, he would take my hand, and we would play for hours outside on his swings. When it got dark, his mother could hear us screaming and pretending to be super-heroes.' She had to call for us to come inside quite often so he could rest. I had wished that sometimes she would let us stay out longer so I could tell him another one of my ghost stories.

One day his mother told me that Luke was getting sicker and had to stay home to get well. He had gotten behind in his class, struggling to keep up with the others. They needed to find him a tutor if his grades did not improve. I did not want to lose him to the fact that he was still behind, so I volunteered to help him get ahead, and soon I became his tutor. When my parents saw me helping him, they knew I had made a true friend. Every day I would make my way over to his house expecting him to let me in. After I rang the doorbell three times the door would open. He wouldn't look into my face because maybe being his teacher embarrassed him. Some days when he didn't want me to help him, I struggled with my patience to teach him. "It's okay," I told him. "Just because you make mistakes doesn't mean I won't like you anymore." However, he didn't like the idea that I was smarter than him. I didn't like seeing him so shameful. However, I already had him under my wings. We had a secret bond of some kind, something that I never could figure out from that first day I met him. He soon forgot his ego and his self-confidence improved.

When it was my tenth birthday my mom held a big party and invited all the neighborhood kids including Luke. When I took him upstairs to my room to show him my new toys, he asked me if he could kiss me on the lips. Shy, I kissed him back. All the kids found out when he had told everyone he had "cooties" and then teased me about it. But I never forgot the best birthday present sitting there among all the others. It was wrapped around a big box. My mom did not want me to open it until everyone else had left. I wondered if it was something my parents would disapprove of. But when I opened the present from Luke, it was an easy bake Betty Crocker oven. I had wanted one for so long but it had always been too costly. The first time I played with it, and baked the chocolate cake, we were so excited to eat it.

Luke had no one else but me in the neighborhood who understood him. When I told my other friends that I wanted to play with him instead they didn't understand. I soon felt that something bad would happen to him if I wasn't there. It was as if he was my own brother and I was trying to protect him. I wasn't sure if it was because I didn't understand our delicate friendship back then or if it was because I liked being motherly to someone. I had wanted someone like him to always be there and I had worried about his health.

We become good friends over those six years of being neighbors. I had fantasized what it would be like if we had gone to the same high school or college. Sadly, his parents were getting a divorce, and my mom told me they were going to move away to Waynesville, Ohio. I had wanted to go back someday to find him but I kept putting it off. When I left home for Providence to go to art school in Minneapolis, it was 1988. My mother had gotten a letter in the mail one day from Luke inviting us to his wedding even though I couldn't attend. I knew that Luke was happily married, had a good job, and was living the life he had always dreamed of. I had been hopeful for his health and whatever happened, I knew that God would provide him a new heart if he needed one.

There was a part of me that had always' wished that life wasn't so vulnerable. But as time stood still, I stared at the old photographs of us in his back yard. I was glad Luke had found someone to love. It was like ripping off a band aid when you just want to keep it on forever, covering up what's already healed.

He didn't need me anymore, even though I never wrote back, I had trusted that we would still meet up someday.

Growing older life teaches you something. That some things can't be brought back, some circumstances can't be prevented, and sometimes no matter how much we want to, we can't fix everything. Sometimes you just have to let things go so they can come back to you. But why do we always try to do everything in our power to control the situation? It's not easy for us to let something else direct our purpose. But how do we trust in a God that takes away what we love the most? Even under circumstances one doesn't understand? Maybe we have to realize that sometimes God doesn't take away that thorn that shakes us. Instead, we must fight it on our own no matter what. Sometimes we need that little shove, and sometimes we need to fail so we can trust something else outside of ourselves. I also knew that God always' give us enough grace to handle whatever battles might come our way.

I remembered that day at the hospital when I had to sign the papers and say goodbye to Phillip. When they turned off the machines, it was difficult to watch the transition. At first his face turned blue, and then his body started convulsing at it ran out of oxygen. The doctor had explained that this was normal when a person is dying. I didn't want to watch it, and I didn't want to see the life inside him die. I had to make that decision forcing me to let go of where I wanted to be, forcing me to want to turn away without him hearing my goodbyes. Sitting in that hospital room I kept thinking we should have waited. "Please God," I prayed, "did I make the right choice?"

I had gotten tired of listening to the echo of the heartbeat on the monitor, it was a sound you never forget. Watching them turn those buttons off felt like something inside my chest had become unplugged too, like an invisible cord cutting off all my oxygen.

I tried not to become angry. When they let me spend our last moments alone, I never wanted it to end. I held Phillip's hand one last time, rubbing the little worn calluses he still had around his knuckles. I thought of a bible verse Eccles 3:1; "To everything there is a season and a time for every matter or purpose under Heaven."

I remembered my father's words as he sat holding onto that steering wheel, his knuckles turning white as we looked ahead waiting for the train to move on. Me sitting next to him as a little girl needing to go to the bathroom. "Be quiet." he would say, "listen to the railroad sing." However, all I heard was the constant banging of the railroad tracks outside. It wasn't fair, we were supposed to die together, me and Phillip, and now here I was facing something inevitable, where I couldn't turn around and change it. I was paralyzed with uncertainty, exhausted, I was a perfect oxymoron; at peace, but in complete utter hell. Somewhere I felt as if some invisible lock had sprung open. I had a sense of letting go of that fear of waiting impatiently for a stupid train. Not knowing what direction, I wanted to take, now I closed my eyes. "It's ok, to let him go." I heard.

Someone had loved me despite every flaw, mistake or imperfection I had. Yet here I was, thinking only of what I wanted and not asking God for help. Maybe, God had spoken to me as I sat there by his bedside at that moment. I squeezed his hand, and I tried to reassure myself to let go because I knew that this was what he would have wanted. Through my tears, I wished he could hear me. Maybe I was hearing things, maybe I was so tired of waiting for that train to finally come to an end so we could just go home. But when I closed my eyes like I had done as a child, I heard the singing this time. "Don't you hear them?" I whispered to Phillip. "They are singing to us; the angels. They are singing just for you." I told him. I wiped the tears from my eyes and heard them so loud and clear. I had hoped he heard the beautiful music too. I thought Phillip had already let go but how would I live again? "Please God." I cried. "How am I going to do this alone?" I was a coward; It takes great courage to let go of what we hold onto the most…

Chapter Seven
(Patty)

The house my best friend Luke had lived in had grown old and it had suffered under its own circumstances. I watched the brown paint wear off the exterior and discolor the window panes, I watched the driveway crack under the black tar melting from the sun, and I watched the trees in the backyard slowly turn brown and die as the branches bent towards the ground. But I knew just like anything in life, the memories it held weren't going to last forever. It was the roots from the trees that grew up around it that caused the most damage my mother had said. There had been a large tree that began to grow up into that house. The roots had threatened to block the pipes underground. That's why no one else had wanted to buy it. In order to save the house, some of the trees around the back had to be destroyed. I remember watching the large bulldozer that had parked in their back yard. I was hoping that they wouldn't destroy anything else. We were glad when the for- sale sign was put back in the front yard. I knew that every house had its layers; each piece was built on top of one another. The frame and inside structure were what held it together. I thought about that house as I looked at it from my fenced in yard. Just because something from the outside threatened to destroy it, didn't mean you had to give up on it.

I was so tired of doubting myself, and chasing the ghost from my past. When you can't trace God's presence or hear his voice, it's easy to pretend he's not there. But here I was at forty -nine hopeful to start over praying every night for direction and wisdom. I knew that my church house would save me from my doubts. I just needed to believe that my faith would get me through it.

On my first day of elementary school, I remember looking out the window of the school bus, as my mother waved goodbye wiping tears from her eyes. Dressed in old summer overalls with a short sleeve shirt from the local thrift store I looked at the other kids all dressed up in name brand jeans and the popular clog sandals. When I looked down at myself, I remember I wasn't going to school to impress anyone; I was there to learn about the world. I held my head high when I was laughed at for carrying so many heavy books across my shoulder during middle school. I wanted to make sure I learned everything well, because I wanted to be prepared for whatever life had in store for me. I had wanted do better so I wouldn't fail. I didn't like the feeling of not being prepared.

In school I had trouble learning numbers in math class and sometimes I would get frustrated and give up on my homework. But my dad had told me; "You need to understand that it's okay to fail and make mistakes so you learn not to do it again." Those times in my life when I had to face those things that made me feel confused it seemed pointless, but we shouldn't let it make us feel stupid, or uncertain just because we can't figure out the algorithm or the reasons why things are the way they are. There are some circumstances that are never meant for us to figure out.

My parents had hoped that as I grew older, I would get some high degree but I wasn't like everyone else. I liked to paint or draw instead. I liked to use my imagination and maybe that was why I worried so much about everything. My mother yelled at me for making a mess with my paints on her new furnished kitchen table. But it was the only way I could express myself when the rest of the world didn't make sense to me. When I showed everyone my drawings even my teachers didn't seem to notice how detailed my pictures were. However, one day Luke saw them and he taped them onto his bedroom window. It made me feel like my art mattered and that was important to me. I had wanted someone to see beneath the mistakes and flaws of what I thought were imperfections. Sometimes when I looked at them, I didn't see my mistakes either.

One day his mother told me they were going to move away closer to a special hospital. I worried that we wouldn't see each other again. I thought Luke was moving just across town and we could visit. However, when my mom told me that they were moving five and a half hours away to Waynesville. I grew anxious as days went by not knowing when they were leaving. It was up to his mother and waiting to see if their present house would sell which never sold.

Luke hadn't quietly grasped what was going on with his parent's divorce and he became guarded. "What's wrong?" I finally asked him one day. He was moody again and couldn't concentrate on his homework.

"I need a sharper pencil this one is pink." He would complain.

I would try to give him a different pencil, and again he complained about something being wrong with it. He would start to fidget and get angry. He finally took the other pencils and broke them, throwing each one across the room. "I hate being sick, now that we have to move away." he finally cried. "You won't be there to play with me anymore."

Finally, I could relate to someone who understood what it was like to be torn apart from something you held so close. "So, you'll miss me?" I asked him. Over that last year we spent together

I never realized that our friendship would become stronger. When it had come to birthday parties, I made sure we celebrated, inviting my friends from the neighborhood. My mother made a great deal over my party because I had been adopted, and Luke of course liked being around all the attention.

I will never forget the day when he wanted to become "blood friends." Luke's sprained arm was still in the sling from falling down my basement steps. An accident one day when we were spooked by a noise that scared us. I wanted us to do it soon because I knew that his parents were talking about moving away. He was thirteen and I was eleven. His mother had run to the store that day and we had some time alone. He found a small army knife and let me lightly cut his finger and then when it was my turn, I couldn't do it I didn't want to feel that pain. "Just don't think about it." He told me. I tried to push the blade deep but then I thought what if I cut too deep? I held the knife close but I was shaking, no blood would come under my skin. I was about to gag when Luke yelled at me. "Hurry up!" he cried and then he grabbed the knife and sliced my finger.

"Ouch you hurt me!" I yelled back as I looked at my throbbing wound. When I saw the blood, he immediately touched my finger. I looked at the blood oozing onto the floor. It was then that I realized that this silly rite of passage meant something between us. His eyes grew wide and big as we stared at the wound.

"I hope this means we will always be connected forever." He said. At that moment I knew that no matter what would happen to us in the future, or where our lives took us, that moment was like an invisible cord. That day marked our trust in each other. When all along I thought it was the end, he had a way of always showing me that it wasn't over yet. As I looked at my scar on my finger years later, I knew that it would always' come back to remind me. What does trust mean between two friends? Does it meaning placing one's confidence in someone hoping they are honest and true? Or does it mean letting them go with the memories you have and letting them come back to you someday?

I was devastated when I found out that Luke and his mother hadn't been home for ten days. No one answered the phone when I called. Did they leave without saying goodbye? Or did something happen to him? I would call his number, then I would go over and knock on the door several times. I panicked when no one answered the door. Fear overwhelmed me when we thought something was wrong. All that time I worried myself to death, thinking I had lost my friend. I had peered inside their windows as days had passed and still no car was in the driveway. I sat on his front steps and waited and hoped. I cried myself to sleep at night wondering if he was dead. We hadn't known that they had just been at the hospital.

When we received the phone call, my mother had said that Luke was okay. He had to have an emergency operation on his heart but was better. All those days I had kept worrying for nothing. I had wondered is this what God must feel like when he is waiting on us? No is home and we are out doing something else not caring about how much he wants to be with us? Giving excuses to tell him to leave a message because your too busy? I didn't like that feeling of ringing the doorbell and waiting for someone to play with.

When that last day came and Luke and I only had a minute to say good bye I was ready this time. I held back the tears and I wanted to show him that I was strong. All that mattered was that we would always be friends. I had never realized how important that was to me until I knew that letting go is not just wrapped up in suffering, but it's needing to say goodbye so you can hold on to those last moments. Sometimes knowing that a part of them lives on, is the only way for you to move forward. I was glad the house next door had reminded me that memories and feelings never change.

After years had passed, I would look out of our top bathroom window of our two-story house and look down to see Luke's backyard with the swing set still in the yard. I had wanted no one else to touch that swing as I watched it blow back and forth in the wind. No one came to buy that house for years or to play in that yard as it sat there and grew old with age. I had wanted so badly to go over there just to sit on that swing again to go back in time to relive those moments as if it was yesterday. It sat there forever, as if mocking the only memory that had abandoned it.

There was something sad but innocent about that empty house even after the trees were removed. However, despite the outside circumstances making it look ugly and vulnerable, it was as if there was a treasure buried somewhere inside it. It had cast a spell over me constantly drawing me towards its shadows. I had wanted to pretend that the house had never aged, and I wanted to pretend that the same house that I had shared with my best friend would stand strong beneath its ghost like frame. I knew that the stories in the depths of its walls wouldn't die. As long as I kept it alive in my mind it would always be there reminding me of its connection.

That little ranch house next door stood still among the memories of dusty polaroid photographs that I had kept away in our old albums. I would often look back and remember my childhood. However, that house was meant to stand strong; as if it was waiting all along for someone like me to accept it underneath all its flaws. Our house stood taller next to it but it wasn't empty and vulnerable like the one standing next to it. In the same way, we might feel inferior, imperfect, or vulnerable but that doesn't mean that we aren't acceptable.

Sometimes it is hard to let go of the things we want to hold onto. As a young girl I felt childish hanging onto so many toys, games, and even records reminding me of my childhood. However, when you get older you realize that you don't need those things anymore. It's hard to give away what you once held so close. I didn't want to get rid of my stuff animals, dolls, or old friendship bracelets reminding me of change. There is a reason why we don't' like change. We like to believe that life has order and is predictable. We want to hold onto the past as if we don't trust the future. No one likes worrying about what tomorrow might hold. The only way to move forward is to close your eyes and remember what you still have.

Chapter Eight
(Patty)

The average person lives 27,375 days. Sometimes I wonder how many of those days do we think back on regrets. How many times do we wonder about I should have, could have, or would have? The good memories that we should hold onto, those are the things that sometimes are the easiest to neglect. However, it's not fair when you sometimes chose to forget the things you should remember. Why do we tend to forget the good things that happen to us and only remember the negative?

At night, I could almost still smell Phillip's Irish spring soap. I could still hear the little snoring sounds he sometimes made, and swear that I could feel the blankets tremble next to me. I wondered if he was really there and this had all just been a bad dream. But in the dark, it's easy to pretend that something is there. The shape of the covers held an empty space, a phantom in the dark… It became a shadow of something that I hadn't wanted to see. If it was too quiet, I would reach over and see if I was just imagining it. I would just tell myself that he was in the living room watching late night tv. But in my mind, I know I am wrong, and that this is real. This time when I reach over to feel the empty spot where he should have been; he is not there.

Sometimes I felt like that abandoned house trying to stand strong among the weeds that threatened it. Those ghosts- like longings of wanting to be accepted wouldn't stop haunting me.

I had wanted God to love me unconditionally and I had wanted to understand who I could be. Consequently, I hadn't realized something; only when you don't embrace God's love, or if you are not reminded day after day that he loves you, it's easy to forget he is there waiting. No matter how unbearable it gets sometimes you must surrender to your own circumstances. It's the only way to keep from looking back and wishing that life was better. Sometimes you have to keep looking at those old polaroid photos, or objects that you keep because it might be the only thing you have left. It reminds you that even though life changes memories never will. You have to keep reminding yourself that it's up to you to keep that place in your heart open because it's the only way to accept the present.

There are so many people who chose death every day; young women getting abortions, terrorist with bombs, doctors preforming euthanasia. Why do so many give up on the choice of life? What is it about death that seems so vain? We struggle to accept our own mortality, we long in vain to reverse death by checking everything we do. Our life is defined by every choice we make. But why do we live life as if it is on some invisible line, constantly worrying about mistakes?

When we look up at the millions of stars around us, you see the layers and patterns of constellations. You know that every star has its place in the sky and every star has its purpose. You trust that what you see is there because of its pattern and where it is. It was something I hadn't thought. Each star's light takes decades to reach earth. When looking at the universe we are always looking back in time itself. Not only are we looking at something that hasn't happened yet, but we trust that it will. The universe teaches us about belief. It teaches us that just because we don't see something doesn't mean it's not there. After most stars die the empty space, it leaves behind, is ninety-nine percent invisible.

I hadn't realized how vulnerable my church looked, sad yet resilient standing alone in the shadows among the clouds; it was so delicate yet strong as it lay under the swaying trees that sheltered it. It had been kept up as it changed over the years but I was going to take care of it now. I remembered the last words my father told me before he had died from his stroke. He hadn't been able to speak much but he could think without reason. "Not everything has a reason to give, sometimes you aren't where you were or wanted to be, nothing ever stays in the lines." Maybe I hadn't wanted to come back, maybe I had been avoiding this town for a reason, but as I think about what I have accomplished so far, I am hopeful that this place will change me. Believing that I could fix it might be challenging but I felt this was where God wanted me to be.

I crawl into my bed and look at Phillips urn on the shelf next to me. Underneath the cold sheets I grew warm. I hoped that with time I would heal. I closed my eyes and thought of my what I still needed to do. Tomorrow, I was going to go down to the police station to see if they had any records about my real mother.

It is morning and as I step into my old Chevy truck, I look over at my church house set back from the road. It was a perfect mirror of what I was. It still had its problem's, the water heater was broken, the plumbing was bad, and my kitchen needed a new floor. Even though it had been remodeled decades ago, it was still looking rough. The roof held patches of plywood covering the small scars from the fire, the front needed painted, and the yard needed trimming. But that was okay because I wanted to make it better. I was hoping to open up the church later on to the community so they could visit and hear the stories of how it survived it's past.

I decide to stop at Marcellas café. It was a small café I had pasted earlier down the street when I moved in. As I drive up to the shop it seems dark from the outside and I wonder if it is open. When I open the door inside it smells of caramel and burnt coffee beans. I look up front by the register but there is no one there. I see a help wanted sign hanging on the door. As I walk in, I get the feeling that maybe it's closed after all. The lights were not all turned on, so I ring the bell sitting up front. I am about to give up and leave when something on the wall catches my eye. "Hello?" I look around and look up to see a picture of a pretty older woman hanging on the wall "Please pray for her recovery." It says underneath. There is a pink cancer ribbon sticking out on the bottom of the frame. As I look closer, I notice her last name, "Marcella Bolan." The name sounded familiar.

Soon I notice an old middle -aged man come out from behind the kitchen door. "I'm sorry, I didn't hear you come in," he apologizes, as he comes out, wiping his hands on a kitchen towel. I feel embarrassed as I ask for a cortado. He flips the lights back on and starts the machine.

"I'm sorry." I apologize looking at the opening time on the door. It was eleven- thirty

"It's Saturday and we don't open until twelve," he hesitates. I look at the menu on the wall, "but that's okay." When I look closer, there is a strange crescent shaped red birthmark on the left side of his face, covered up by a grey beard and glasses. He seems to not notice me as he disappears to go to in the back. I am shocked and suddenly realize that he looks like Luke my childhood friend from long ago. He is gone for a while and as I wait and listen to the clock above me, I look at the picture of the woman in the frame again. Of course, I had forgotten about the wedding invitation so long ago. She was his wife. Oh my, I think. It's Luke.

When he comes back, he rings up my cortado and grabs my money. It is suddenly quiet and I anxiously look toward the clouds through the window. I am so shocked and excited that I don't say anything at first. I grab my phone and try to look for a picture of my old house from Providence. He probably wouldn't recognize me at forty-nine. "You look familiar, did you ever live in Providence?" I anxiously ask.

He looks down as if he doesn't hear me and hesitates. "Yes, when I was young, until we moved here where I met my wife, but she's gone now, she died of breast cancer two months ago."

"Oh, I'm so sorry." I awkwardly watch him pour my drink and am so mesmerized by his slow sharp movements. I look towards the door but outside it has started to rain. "I'm sorry, but do you remember a girl who used to live next door to you in a yellow house?" I ask him hoping I didn't sound crazy.

He finally looks up at me as if he had seen a ghost. "Patty?"

"Yes, I thought it was you, how are you?" I look over my bifocals at him again as I sit down with my drink. I had thought I was dreaming again.

"Haven't seen your face for decades, what are you doing in this part of town?" he finally asks. I suddenly feel a rush of adrenaline, there was something about the way he asked me.

"I just bought the St Lindon's Catholic church on Parson's St a month ago. I wanted to get away from Providence where I grew up and come back here. You remember the story about my birth mother and how she had died after she left me at the church? But here I am now, when four months ago, I was in a severe car accident. I survived but my husband passed." I sadly reply. I take a sip of my drink and hide my face in the hot steam.

"Oh, I'm so sorry. Why didn't you contact me?" He seems curious, and then he asks me, "So, were you hurt? It must have been very traumatizing?"

I start to tell him my story of how my husband had died from brain damage due to his coma. I explain that due to the bad weather and that it was his birthday I felt guilty about the accident. I had only sustained a concussion, and a sprained wrist, but he had hit his head on the windshield. "It probably was my fault; I should not have started the argument that distracted him." I explain. For some reason my tiredness has gotten the best of me but when I look up after I have wiped my eyes, I realize that he has disappeared to the back again. "I'm sorry, I didn't mean to upset you." "Luke...?" but he doesn't seem to notice. He goes to the back and I hear him washing dishes avoiding me for some reason. This was not the same person I had known before. I wanted to catch up on his life but I hadn't known about his wife Marcella who had recently died. Maybe he just needed time and me reminding him of what he had lost was too much. I quietly get up to leave as it has started to thunder outside.

The rain has turned into a windy storm blowing the trees and soon the sky is grey. I start my truck and head home. It was only ten minutes away. I think about the state Luke was in; he was still grieving. But something was different this time. It was like he didn't really remember me. I was hoping he would tell me more about his life and I wanted to know about how his health was. I was wondering how he would handle this coffee shop on his own. Suddenly I felt sorry for leaving him all alone. Outside the rain stops for a moment, and I am tempted to turn around to go back and ask him if he wanted to talk about it. I remembered his brown eyes and scarlet moon shaped birthmark that ran down the left side of his chin. He was older but still looked the same. Luke had been the only person growing up who understood the loss I had felt for my birth mother. I sit in my car thinking again; his brown hair underneath the white, his familiar brown eyes behind his glasses, and I hadn't even realized that it was him at first.

Me and Luke had grown up during the seventies when the Rolling Stones and Bee Gees were popular. Those were the days when we thought that life like this would last forever. It was fun to dancing to the music. I thought we were invincible and nothing could take away our security of tomorrow. Now here we were, losing what we had held on so tightly, and still not knowing where we were going.

The clouds break and it soon stops to a light patter. I turn back onto the long road that leads me home. Behind my windshield, I look out over the dreary scene before me. I pass block after block of run-down buildings, vacant stores, and broken sidewalks. So many places here looked well past age with sagging porches, yards choked with weeds and rotting trash cans in the back. I did not know why I had wanted to move to Waynesville. Maybe I felt I needed a refining of my past, because I had felt this place held a part of my past too. Maybe I felt neglected and ignored, like this old town with its broken- down buildings and old antique malls. Maybe I needed to find a reason why a place like this can offer nostalgia when I had thought it was gone. From the beginning life had taught me that sometimes chaos can redirect us to find the direction we should be going.

My house had once been a Catholic church, the same church where I had been abandoned. I didn't like the thought of being left at that church. It made me feel as if I wasn't meant to be with a family where I felt loved or accepted. There were so many reasons for me to justify why these things kept holding me down. I didn't want to face the loss and knowing that such a tragedy had happened to my mother. I hadn't really known Father Eugene, the man whom had taken me to social services that day but I was grateful for the parents who had given me a new beginning.

I imagined what might have gone on behind these church walls, funerals, weddings, Eucharist,' and confessions. Long veils brushing the bottom of the floor as the bride walked out to start her new life, funeral caskets being closed as they were taken to the back, the sound of tears crying over a loved one. So many memories it must have held. So many people had come here looking for answers to whatever they were going through. How many had come looking for redemption? How many had believed but then felt like me, when something terrible had happened that God had forgotten them leaving them stranded? I had sometimes felt lost too.

Had I been lying to myself all this time, pretending to believe in my faith just to give me a security in the cruel world that had surrounded me? Was I using my religion to protect me from getting hurt? Sometimes we must remind ourselves daily that God is not all about rules and commandments. Consequently, when I was little, to me my belief in God was supposed to teach me that he would always protect me from all the terrible things in life. I was supposed to enjoy reading my Bible and learn from the stories of how God's people weren't perfect. Those people needed God not just for redemption but for peace and guidance. Good and evil are not absolute, because the devil exists, there will always be bad things in this world. Man was created to be imperfect and sinful so we could rely on him through our suffering. In the same way, we learn to become selfless and forgiving.

I had felt that I had spent my whole life looking for my purpose in the universe. I kept questioning what does God want me to do? Was the life I was living for myself or was I living for him? Why couldn't I feel satisfied? Sometimes we miss the most important part of what we cannot see. It's so easy to rely on facts, evidence and what you think is true. However, it only takes a little faith to believe in miracles.

§

Chapter Nine
(David)

David had been hiding in his office at the St Mary's Catholic church since seven am. He would start early every morning and arrive at six. Before the phone calls started and the paper work for his sermon needed to be done, he had always liked the quietness of the early part of the day. It gave him time to reflect and think on spiritual matters. At sixty-seven he was getting older and hoped to retire soon. He wished he could rewrite his past without all the dark parts, to unknow the things he knew, and to unsee the things he'd seen.

David looked out his window, he couldn't concentrate. He put down his pencil, rubbed his eyes, and felt the breeze of the small fan behind his desk on his neck. He thought of the fire from the St Lindon's church back on that warm April night of 1992. He had seen the smoke coming from the church from across the street. He had been getting gas at the gas station that night filling up his black ford mustang. He had been forty -seven back then and he was on his way to a sabbatical retreat. When he turned around, he saw a familiar man come running towards him. He also had been there and saw the smoke. He had pointed across the street as they saw that Father Eugene's car was in the parking lot. He had been the only one still there after Mass that evening. When they ran over to the church, they knew that Father Eugene was trapped inside.

David still remembered telling the other man, to not go inside until the firetrucks came. However, they had waited as the town gathered around the scene deciding what to do. David watched as the flames spread and into the windows. The other man finally went inside the burning building, and didn't come out for some time. David didn't know what to do as he watched the fire spread up towards the roof. The firetrucks had taken a long time to arrive, and he remembered waiting and watching in shock. When they saw the roof cave in, David knew that the men inside might not make it out. Some nearby neighbors had gathered around the church and prayed. As they watched the firetrucks extinguish it the medics tried to save them. David was able to help pull the men out from under the pile quickly but both were unconscious. Father Eugene had died as he was taken to the hospital where he had suffered severe injuries from a concussion. David rode with the medics hoping that the other man would make it, praying on the way. He hadn't known the man Luke well, but he had remembered him from St Lindon's as a young boy.

When they had arrived at the hospital, they told him that Luke's heart was too weak to do surgery on his burns that needed taken care of. David was told that the heart had weakened due to a lifelong defect with his heart. Luke had stopped breathing the next day and the life support had been the only thing keeping him alive until his organs were donated. David had left that day dismayed as it had all come falling out from under him. The news had described Luke as a hero for risking his life, but losing it to save another. However, David had hoped he could have prevented such a tragedy.

The town never forgot the sad loss of Father Eugene and Luke. The church was recovered and closed down due to the terrible accident. The investigation later had found no cause of the fire. The only evidence was some candles left on the alter that might have fallen over. They had possibly caught onto the curtains that went upwards to the vaulted roof. Due to the burning points on the floors, it did not look like someone had done it on purpose.

David had been a priest at St Mary's down the street when the congregation from St Lindon's started going to his church. It was as if they had come to him seeking for answers and questioning why. He had tried to mend the broken hearted, the hurt, and the anger that they carried. He felt he was the only one they had looked up to, when he tried to give the town the promises of Gods strength and hope. David had tried to explain reasons as to why God lets bad things happen to good people, but he never could find the answers himself. He would drive by the old church sometimes and look into the windows of the empty deserted building and remember those he had once known. He never forgot that day Father Eugene had found someone's baby lying inside a box, not knowing why anyone would do such a thing. Not too long ago he had seen a "For Sale" sign in the yard. He had wished he had the money himself to buy it when he wondered if it would ever become a church again.

At night David could feel something watching him. Sometimes he could feel the sadness as it crept into his mind. He hated facing the reality that sin was the result of death. It terrified him, and watching those that he knew suffer in front of him, only made him question his own faith even more. The people in his congregation had always wanted him to give them assurance. But did he have all the answers? Was the Bible absolute proof? Did it have enough evidence that there is a place we go to when we die?

For so long he had believed he could save people from there hopelessness. He was supposed to protect this town from its hate and anger. From their racial prejudice to their condemning political harassment's, they had looked up to him for support and faith. As a young boy his mother had told him to say the rosary every night, as she prayed for peace over his sins. But he had failed at being the person God had wanted him to be. He followed all the commandments of his faith but he still felt he couldn't give enough of his promises to the God he had believed in. Something was still holding him back. He held his mask tight, it was his comfort zone, and that's what kept him from feeling anything when he kept his secrets close.

They thought that because he was a priest that he was supposed to set an example of holiness. But the truth was he had been living his whole life under a lie. When he had his heart broken by the love of his life was when he really started questioning everything. Before he had become a priest, he had a different life and had planned on marrying. He had missed Mary and his daughter he never got to know. He played the only card he had saved, the ace he held so close for so many years. Consequently, holding on to something he couldn't bear to lose, that was his weakness. He had thought he was strong, that he could overtake those demons, but he didn't like appearing weak. His anger had always gotten the best of him causing him to fail. He couldn't just hide from it; it was eating him up from somewhere deep inside. He knew he kept blaming himself for not looking for the baby that was given a new home. He wasn't sure if it had mattered because Mary was gone. He didn't want to tell his daughter how her mother had so many problems. David had hoped to look up the information, and he had planned on doing it, but then later had become never. He had gotten too busy again taking care of the church.

David looked down at his orange tabby cat Red, she was the only thing at this moment in his life that relied on him. It was nice to feel like something belonged to him in his lonely old house. His mother had known that her son had wanted to become the father that he had always wanted to be. However, he had wanted to face those monsters that even she couldn't face, and she wanted him to become the godly person that he was meant to be. Still after a year later they kept growing more apart. They couldn't forget what had happened. He had hoped that he could move on, but he had felt sorrowful as the years went by.

In his eyes he wanted to be the catalyst, because he wanted to believe that life wasn't held by such a delicate thread. He hadn't realized that sometimes we don't get second chances. However, David had been playing his cards wrong all along. He never needed to redeem himself just because he felt overwhelmed when trying to help those he loved. Being a priest had been his kryptonite making him feel vulnerable but appearing strong from the outside. But sometimes when you play with a joker card, and you wait too long; you bluff. That was the mistake he made when he didn't go after Mary that night. On the other hand, he thought he could trust her.

That next day Sarah had told him what happened as she cried into his arms. "Oh, my God she's gone," his mother had told him. "Mary told me she wanted to go to Providence for rehab and juvenile. We were going to meet at the train station. However, she had gotten upset and changed her mind, she said she couldn't do it. I think she needed your support before she left."

"What happened?" David had asked her. He grew suspicious when she somehow had turned up with the rosary, and had lied to the police about being home that night when he knew she had not been home. In fact, when questioned, she told them that she was at home watching TV that night. Everyone knew that Mary was overcoming her addiction and most had believed that she had just run away. His mother was the only one who knew what had really happened. David didn't know if he should have gone to the police when he noticed something strange on his mother's car the next day. The front bumper had a large dent in it as if she had hit something. But just like some games there are always repercussions to justify when you must finally give in, you can't bluff over the joker card for too long when you're the one holding the ace…

🎵

Chapter Ten
(Patty)

I have decided I had wanted to stop in Providence, Kentucky to go back home for a couple days. I wanted to visit my old neighborhood again. It had been over thirty years since I had been to my old house. I wanted to remember it because I still felt the accident had taken some memories away. I thought it would help me get over my loss.

When I was getting my art therapy degree, I was glad I was learning to help someone someday. In class I was told by my teachers to stop following so many rules. I was told to move away from the shape, size and details. But I needed to use a ruler sometimes, in order to get the outlines right. Before putting it on canvas, I would erase and erase my mistakes. I couldn't stop worrying about the crooked lines and the outcome. For me abstract art was intensely hard because I didn't want to create something unrealistic or imperfect. I wanted the object I drew to be something that I was familiar with, so the observer could figure it out. I had wanted them to accept my painting with no mistakes. I found it easier to follow the rules when there was an image or guide to follow. On the other hand, I couldn't just draw from memory, I didn't trust it.

Sometimes the things that we hold back from ourselves, get in the way of finding our true self. The fact is, it weakens our minds because we think it defines us. We think that we aren't strong enough to handle our failures and so we pretend that there is nothing wrong. We stay behind our comfort zone but unhappy of where we are.

I remember how much trouble I had during my first art class. I had always thought my drawings had to be realistic and look exactly like what I wanted. But most art has to be something mysterious and terrifying, uncanny or repulsive so one can guess and really look at it to find the true meaning behind its story. Why is it so hard for us to feel vulnerable and free and to let that part of ourselves go? Why do we set limits as if there is someone waiting to punish us? Sometimes just drawing on a blank sheet of paper I would stare into space, I had the pencil in my hand ready to draw, but I froze every time. The fact is it's hard to be perfect with art because we worry that if we reveal all our insecurities that what others see might not be accepted.

My art teacher told me that a painter doesn't create with his hands but with his eyes, and what he wants people to know about himself. If my art looked imperfect that was okay because people look for blemishes, space, and disposition. All along my ideas were there but like a puzzle I had to find the missing pieces inside myself. In the same way, if you try to let go, it can become something abstract forcing the observer to look beyond what's inside the lines. Real art is hard to accomplish because the only way for it to become good is if it shows its pain, its past, and everything that hides beneath, not the perfect details we see on the outside. "It's a lie that tells the truth," As Picasso once said. Art is full of doubts, flaws, and secrets. It's what people look for because that's what they need. In the same way, we all need to understand that life is not perfect. When you can go back again and again to the same picture, and find a different perspective or angle of that piece, then it no longer is just art but something else in disguise.

It is late once I arrive in Cincinnati and look for a motel. I was going to stop sooner but I didn't want to drive the next three and half hours. I walk inside up to the front desk of the motel and check in for the cheapest single bed. I drag myself to the elevator to the second floor, unlock the door with the card, and turn on the lights but then the bulb blows out. I stand there for a moment trying to decide if I should go back down to complain. But I am too tired. There is another light in the bathroom, so I find my way with the streetlights coming in through the window. I could have gone back down to tell them I want another room, but I didn't want to bother them about it. From the light of the bathroom, I can see enough to unpack and change into my night clothes. The roads had been wet with rain and a storm had blown through hours before. I take my phone, and put it by the bedside table.

Suddenly, in the early morning I am awakened by my phone ringing next to me. I suddenly jerk up realizing where I am; I reach for it. "Hello?" I answer with a raspy tired voice. "Hello?" It is quiet on the other line as I wait. I finally hang up wondering who it was. My phone had caller ID but does not notice the number.

After I pack my bags, I walk back down to the empty lobby, it seems dark as if the electricity had been out. As I step out of the elevator and pull my suitcase down the hall, I have the strange feeling that someone is watching me. I stop and look around but see nothing. I look at the snack machine and see the Natures Valley granola bar, but as I dig into my purse, I realize that I have left my wallet in the room. As I go back into the elevator, I notice that I am the only one on the floor. It seemed strange and quiet. Where is everyone? I think. I finally make it back down to the front desk, but no one is there. I look around nervously, I had already paid online but needed to check out. "Hello?" I look for a bell to ring. It was still early and I wondered if the desk was open yet. There is a chill in the lobby with the same eerie feeling that someone is watching me. I wait for a couple minutes to see if anyone else is around. These cheap hotels seem so abandoned that nobody likes them, I think to myself. I walk out the door and jump into my truck wondering if I had forgotten anything.

It was after my papaw had died when I was nineteen, but I didn't know much about death back then. I told my mother I didn't want to go to the funeral because I didn't like them. I believed that the soul lives on after one dies and finds peace in Heaven. Why go and mourn over a loss when that person is finally at peace? I didn't see the point in staring at a dead body lying in a casket. I on the other hand, hadn't wanted to face the reality of the happiness that can be taken from you. I wasn't sure if it was fear, or if I just didn't want to believe that everyone wasn't invincible.

I remembered something my mother had asked me before she passed; "Make sure you come to my funeral; it would be a terrible party without you. It's okay to mourn over a loss. It helps us remember what's left behind." I started going to more funerals after that even though I hated them. On the other hand, my mother couldn't teach me about one thing; "There are no such things as monsters," she had said. But she never warned me about the ones that could come out of nowhere, sitting under your security waiting to take away what you thought was true. There will always be conflicts we must face, and I by now knew that no matter how much power it has over you, sometimes you have no other choice but to find within yourself, that shelter. When you don't know what to do, you question yourself about what's holding you back.

When I closed my eyes at night to go to sleep, I always prayed a special prayer for those I missed or lost. I imagined my adoptive mother now looking down at me from Heaven. She had died later from Alzheimer's and had been a strong Christian. She had believed in God, going to church and following in her faith. However, she had forgotten who I was and my father who had died years before. She liked to talk about the good old days and remember good times. However, she never forgot about where she would be going after she died. She looked forward to that place called Heaven as if she was going on some long vacation. She even had her bags packed when hospice came to be with her. I smile as I remembered her waiting as if it was the only thing she had wanted to talk about. She had missed my father and that's why she had wanted to go. That's what kept her believing until the end. They had loved each other and she knew he was waiting for her in Heaven.

We all have secrets and things that we don't want to face but that's because we are human. They say negative moments are remembered, but traumatic ones are forgotten. Something happened to me that caused me to forget some details after Phillip died. I don't remember going to the funeral. They said the bump on my head had caused amnesia and would take time for me to heal. The funny thing was I kept having the same dreams every night but I remembered them. First, I am on a bridge looking down at a lake. A bright light shines in my face making me pass out. Then as I open my eyes and look down, I am floating high above the ceiling in some room. There are people surrounding someone lying in a hospital bed as they are connected to some machines. I can't see the persons face underneath, but this time I can hear them, they were saying my name, and they were praying for me. It was me lying asleep, unknown to the world in that bed.

Chapter Eleven
(David)

David never forgot the day when they were informed that his dad had been shot in Vietnam. He was just finishing seminary school when they had received the terrible news from a letter in the mail. It was 1968 and his mother sat down to anxiously read him the letter. She had started to cry, as she angrily tore up the small note. But like many others who had been lost in battle, his father had been a true hero in his eyes. He went without fear, did his best, and faced his enemy until the end.

David hated the war and had wished for it to end. Maybe he did blame it for his father's death. The thought of loving someone so much that you hate them for dying and leaving you, left him empty. He just couldn't face the fact that he never got to know his real father. He had grown used to hearing about the war all over the radio. It had been a terrible situation that had affected them all. So many innocent people were being killed. So many were hoping for peace yet they thought fighting was the answer. Back then he didn't give a care about what happened. The problem was both sides couldn't forgive and they couldn't stop hating each other. The truth was they had hoped all along that peace was the solution.

David remembered how Mary's body was found. Her body was retrieved weeks later under the bridge. The last time he had seen her was that night at the church. It was the same bridge he had drove on every day to get home. The autopsy performed could not distinguish if it had been a suicide, homicide, or accident. The investigation had found multiple injuries to her body including a broken neck. They also could tell that it hadn't happened recently. David and his mother had been questioned. Beforehand, his mother had turned in a rosary she said she had found by the bridge. He had told the authorities that he had spoken with Mary that day at the church, and that she had told him she was heading towards the train station. His mother, on the other hand told them she found a train ticket in Mary's room weeks before. She suspected Mary was planning on going to Providence where the family who had her baby lived.

The authorities worked hard in questioning witnesses as to what had happened. No one had seen Mary on the bridge that night. David had thought his mother was hiding something. Finally, there was another witness from a friend at their church. She had told them that Mary told her that she was going to meet someone at the train station that day. David knew that he had a reputation in town and people knew they were friends. He had worried that it all looked suspicious. When he took his mother's old green Ford Escort in to get it fixed one day, he had found Mary's red sweater in her trunk. When questioned his mother had told him that Mary must have left it there the last time she had borrowed her car. Even more strange was she had lied to the police about where she was that night. Was his mother hiding something? The case was closed when no evidence could prove if someone had thrown her body into the lake or if she had fallen.

David knew that Mary had wanted to live. Had he been wrong all along about how delicate she was? He had hoped she wanted a better life. He should have known better to get involved with someone like her. He also knew that his mother kept getting in the way. He didn't want Mary's problems to get them into trouble but it seemed as if there was no way around it. David's heart sank as he thought about how they could have helped her.

All that time it was if he was a puppet on a string pretending to become something that he wasn't. He had wanted to be a father because he wasn't good at being a priest. He felt like he was punishing himself all the time wondering what other life he could have had. He was planning on going back to Providence to find his daughter someday. He had wanted to meet the girl that had caused so much heartache. He wanted to tell her about her mother and the special woman she was. He was sure the adoptive family hadn't revealed much detail about it to her. He didn't want her to grow up knowing that her mother had abandoned her. On the other hand, he never could make himself admit that he needed to do this for his own good someday. Didn't his daughter deserve to know that she had a father who had wanted to meet her and ask for forgiveness for not being there?

David sat at his kitchen table and poured himself another cup of coffee. He never slept well but he liked to get up early in the morning. He thought that most people were like pawns on a chessboard moved by an unknown hand. That every bad choice was the result of one's separation from sin. Sometimes he wondered if life was really predetermined. He remembered something his teachers taught him in school in Physics it was about the Quantum theory of science. When it comes down to it, most objects never stay separate for long, because when you drill down to the core of the most solid material, separateness always dissolves. All that remains are the particles of atoms of whatever is left through space and time. In the same way, the microscopic world of molecules somehow become entangled within the universe, giving connections to every lost data as if frozen in time. It gave him a reason to believe that everything is connected even when it is not physically there. He always felt that he was connected to something greater.

David got up to reach the top shelf in the closet where he kept the locked box. He did not forget the combination; he stared at the shiny nine-millimeter gun. He only kept it for emergencies just in case. There had been a couple of break-ins around town recently. It had only been used once, during the years he had moved into his mother's house. There was a stray black shepherd that kept coming around. It would come onto the porch at night and scratch at the door. He really bought the gun to just use it to scare the dog away, but every night she still came back. The poor old dog was scared but she wanted food. It was like she had chosen them to test them to see if they would accept its vulnerability, its hunger, and its need to feel wanted. She was skittish at first, but soon gained his trust. His mother soon realized how gentle the dog was and they named her Mercy. She gained weight and soon began to trust them letting him take her on daily walks. He remembered her soft thick black fur and how she would roll onto the ground and let him rub her stomach.

One morning he couldn't find her when he left the house to get firewood. That cold winter day he had searched the woods all afternoon walking through the falling snow. It was below freezing and she was old. He walked towards the back trails then soon enough he saw something up ahead; it was a fallen dead tree that had blocked an icy creek. Inside the old rotted walnut tree lying on the ground was the dog. She lay cold as ice on her side as if she had chosen her place to die. That's when he realized that she had wanted to be alone so she could be at peace. That dog had been through a lot before it had found them; and he knew she had been fragile. David wondered why Mercy had wanted to die alone.

In the same way, he did not want to think about how Mary must have felt. She had wanted someone to rescue her. She had wanted him to accept her for the ugly mess she had gotten into. Her demons had haunted her as if it didn't recognize who she was becoming. Consequently, he couldn't see that the monster that kept her prisoner had destroyed him too. He had felt helpless as he tried to reason with her in the church that night. He knew that even the cold dark emptiness of death, could never be worse than facing those he couldn't save…

Chapter Twelve
(Patty)

I finally arrive in Providence, Kentucky and drive the back way to the road and turn up on the hill to McKinley Dr as I head towards my old neighborhood, I feel like I am in some nostalgic dream. I wanted to see Luke's house and was sure someone had been living there all those years. All I could do was be spiteful and hope that everything was the same as I had remembered it.

The day after my childhood friend had moved to Waynesville it kept haunting me as if it wouldn't go away. I kept thinking of ways to get there. I kept wondering why I didn't return to that small town. I kept worrying that I didn't want to move too far away from the parents who had adopted me. I don't know why I kept avoiding it, when I kept thinking I would go back later when I was ready. However, when you tell yourself later, later becomes never.

I turn on Bluegrass dr and park on the opposite side of the rode and see the address 5618, and then I see my two-story yellow house sticking out behind the large maple tree, the one my dad had planted in the front yard when I was ten. I stare at the car parked in the driveway. The house my parents lived in still looks well kept. There is a new tire swing in the front tree and the same rusty metal fence surrounding the backyard. I was glad someone lived there. Next to it is the brown, grey, and black checkered brick ranch house the one Luke had lived in. I look closer, there is no evidence of a car there, but the yard looks well-kept and there is a welcome cat decoration on the door. It is enough evidence that someone is there.

I hold back the tears I had been keeping so deeply inside. It all comes back to me. You don't realize how much you could care about someone until they are gone. Why did it make me feel so sad? I walk over to the fenced in yard among the new trees covering the back. I look for the old swing set but it is no longer there. It was as if it was the only thing that connected me to my childhood. Now that it was gone, I felt a deep loss. Why do the ones we care about cause so much heartache and pain after their gone? I felt angry. I look at my wedding ring on my hand and took it off. "Why me God?" I ask. I didn't need anything to remind me, but why couldn't I let it go?

I get back to my car and think of something my mother had told me. "Some people pass and go into our lives, some become just a memory, and if your lucky some become a part of who you are." She was right maybe I needed something like this to help me understand it. I hadn't realized the answer had been right there all along, I just was looking at life from the wrong angle. Looking at the house from the back the yard it was unkept as it held so many more abandoned memories and truth, but looking at the house from the front you would have never guessed that it was as strong as it was. You would never have guessed that it carried a story, about two childhood friends, who spent day after day dreaming of dreams that gave birth to hope. Maybe all along I just needed that promise. I was reminded by a Bible verse. Isaiah 40:31; "But those who wait on the Lord shall renew their strength. They shall mount up with wings like eagles, they shall run and not be weary, they shall walk and not faint."

I look around and I can still smell the sweet lavender lilac trees, I can still taste the sweet lemonade on my mouth, and I still could hear us laughing and tasting the warm afternoon rain. I peek over the house again and know that it was always meant to be remembered this way. It made me feel young again as if my own life hadn't started yet. I sighed, I was forty-nine but nothing hadn't changed, I had. Life had gotten in the way because it does. I had grown stronger learning to face my setbacks and circumstances. I had missed my best friend but now it was time for me to say goodbye to another. "God?" I cried. "I know it's been a long time, but please forgive me for not trusting in you. You, were always' waiting for me to come back. I thought I didn't deserve your forgiveness." I pause and smile, the most important lesson I took with me after Luke had moved away, was trust. When you trust someone with all your heart, there will always be an open door, no matter what you have done. It's never too late. Likewise, God is always waiting for us to come back and knock on his door. It's our choice to trust that he will always be there to let us in.

Chapter Thirteen
(David)

David looked at the shadow of light coming in from his bedroom window. It seemed to bring out the baby blue paint that he had painted decades ago. He knew that when light fell on an object, the surface had a particular way of absorbing the wavelengths of the spectrum and when reflected back to your eyes it became whatever color you see. But how does one really see color? There were so many reasons that sometimes he only noticed greys, underneath a world full of color. He never let himself see those bright and healthy spectrums, because he didn't want to believe they were there. He just couldn't get outside of himself to see that shadow and light can never separate. But what happens when you can't separate the invisible from the visible? He had been taught that human nature was always looking for its other half, because it cannot be separated from itself. In the same way, he knew that sometimes you cannot separate goodness from evil; they always shared a single root.

David thought about how he wished he could forget. Was that how it should feel? As if it was some forgotten chapter in some dark corner of his mind collecting dust, and covering the things of what lay hidden underneath? He had known that Mary was a strong believer. He had thought he could help her follow God and become the mother she was meant to be. She had told them that she didn't want to go back to rehab. She thought she could do it all on her own. He had thought that if she stayed around longer, instead of running away, that they could give her some encouragement. However, she didn't see the fairness in the family, who had tried to keep her away from their new baby. The problem was Mary was stuck. She couldn't move forward and she couldn't go back. David had no other choice but to give in when she wouldn't listen to his advice. David hadn't wanted to think otherwise. In his mind, he thought it was a suicide. On the other hand, that's what he told anyone who had asked him, he told them Mary had died of a broken heart.

David thought of the day she had told him that she was pregnant and how he had been shocked. He was planning on becoming a priest. He couldn't be a father or marry, and she wasn't well enough to be a mother. They had argued about her choice for an abortion. But she had grown angry at him and had wanted to keep the baby. He felt bad now when he thought about it. Maybe she wouldn't have felt so stressed if she had. He had wished he could take it all back and start over. He had wanted to save her but he couldn't tell her how much he had loved her.

David looked out his kitchen window. He sometimes wished that his call to God hadn't interfered. His past held so many hopes under his secrets, so many truths under it's lies, and so many answers under his questions. Sometimes he felt like the superhero fighting against right and wrong. But how could he try to point a finger at his congregation when he was guilty of his own misdirection? The fact was, he felt that he was not worthy to ever be a priest when he couldn't repent of his own transgressions.

He remembered when his mother had gotten the brain cancer diagnosis a year later. The doctors had said the mass had spread and there was nothing they could do. He stayed over in the hospital for weeks, and he would hold her hand after the chemo.

She would become so nauseas and sick as she took the medicine. He would sit in the chair by her bedside day after day. Then she would tell him to go home, as she closed her eyes and fell asleep. But he couldn't, he didn't want to go back to the house all alone. However, he had prayed for her to get well, but she believed she wouldn't. That's what tore him apart the most, he couldn't win. The cancer had finally consumed her, and there was nothing they could do. He thought she would suffer under her circumstances but as he watched her laying so peacefully in bed, she didn't seem to fight it, she just surrendered. It was as if she had been waiting all along to let the cancer consume her, as if she had wanted to die. He remembered the way she had looked into his eyes as she questioned him. "Son, is repentance enough?" she had asked him.

David didn't have an answer as he held his tongue. "It's impossible to place your faith in God without changing your mind about your sin. It's not work that earns your salvation." He had told her. "But Mary's death was nobody's fault." He had reminded her. "Please stop blaming yourself." When she told him how she had felt it was her fault that Mary had jumped over the bridge, she thought she would go to Hell no matter what. When David had questioned her again there was something else she couldn't tell him. It seemed she wasn't just sorrowful but she was shameful, as if she had been hiding something from him for a long time. "Where were you that night that you didn't come home?" he had asked her. She had just told him she had been staying at a friend's house.

There were times when he had wanted to know what it was like to be a father. To have someone to care about and give advice too. David had tried to be a good man when he thought he had followed all the commandments. It was hard to do the sacrament of baptism of the babies when a family wanted it done. He would often look at the crying child he had held in his arms and wonder about his own. He had only gotten the chance to hold his child at the hospital. It made him feel guilty for ignoring it because he knew there was something still unfinished yet to do in his life.

David wished he could go back to his childhood when he had played with fireflies at night. He didn't squish them between his fingers or trap them in a jar to suffer like some of the other boys did; instead, he cupped them in his hand for a moment and whispered, "Go find your way home." He knew that even God's insects had a purpose somewhere on earth. He had hoped that his daughter would find her place in the world like that firefly, and if she had gotten lost along the way, then she wouldn't feel trapped in the in between, where he sometimes felt separated from God.

One thing he knew was that his faithfulness was growing old and tarnished, as if hidden away behind some curio cabinet. He was tired of looking at the same painting in his office that still hung on his wall above his desk. It was an old painting of "Jacob's ladder." Jacob was on his knees looking upward towards the dark sky. His face showed astonishment but fear as he looked upwards towards the ladder coming out of the clouds. He knew that the painting could represent many things. The ladder was to symbolize the separation between God and man. It was the gap of Heaven and Hell created by sin. But the ladder was also a covenant made for man so he could exchange his sins for righteousness. Jacob was trying to find his way back to God. It was from Genesis 28: 10-19. David had looked at that painting so many times. He had feared God, knowing that sometimes his choices resulted in his guilt. However, he wondered; what holds man back from absolution? Was it lack of trust or fear? What was it about sin that caused one to be so complacent?

9

Chapter Fourteen
(Patty)

I had left that hospital without my husband, and not knowing where to go from where I was in my life, I didn't want to go back to the same house. There were to many memories of seeing his old leather recliner sitting in the corner of the living room, or smelling his stinky towel still hanging in the bathroom. Staring at those forgotten photographs of someone you lose you want to shove them into your old shoeboxes' as if it doesn't matter. I felt like I should put our whole life away into some computer file as if I didn't want to retrieve it again.

Maybe I was never really good at letting go of unfulfilled expectations. Sometimes you just want to hold onto an apple and smell it, but you don't want to eat it. You know that its sweet fragrance means it's good and ripe, but if you bite into it, you wonder if it will taste as good as you want. I felt like I wasn't letting myself have that sweetness out of the life that I had wanted because I kept worrying that it wouldn't be enough. I thought the goodness of life would be taken if I stepped outside of my comfort zone, and all that would be left was the inner core stained with the brown rotting of indigence. But the fact was, I should have taken more chances. I should have bit into that apple and torn it apart with my teeth, it didn't matter if it wasn't going to last.

There was a time when I thought that I would never find someone to love me. You start to wonder about your place, your purpose, and if things could have been different. Sometimes I had wondered what my life would have been without Phillip. Would I have found someone different but unhappy? Would I have stayed single but still searching? I look at the unopened pile of mail on my kitchen table. I had appointment to meet with some investigators down at the police station next week. I wasn't sure how much information they would have, but I was hopeful they would find the files about my mother. I had nothing of who she was only a name.

I sit in my living room and look out my window, I remembered a time when Phillip and I had to put our black cat Blue to sleep. He was twelve years old by then, and his condition had gotten worse, giving him severe asthma, causing him great distress in breathing affecting his heart. There was no medicine or procedure they could use to help him. We sadly watched him lose weight and he wasn't able to care for himself anymore even though he still held on. It was Phillip's decision to take him to be euthanized. I had thought it was wrong and that we should let the poor cat die at home. But he had said the cat was in pain and 'shouldn't we make the rest of his time less stressful?' We had argued over it until I gave in. I couldn't even go with him when he took Blue to the vet. I didn't like the thought of putting him to sleep as if we were killing him. Why did we have to choose? That poor cat was my friend and I just didn't want to see him go. I had cried knowing that Phillip was right. It's not fair to make one suffer under life's circumstances, when something can be done to end its pain. On the other hand, it doesn't feel any better, when you must help something die because it can no longer handle those circumstances on its own.

When I was twelve, I went into my parent's bedroom during a bad storm and my mother let me sleep in their bed. My father had been working late. I caught her crying when I had opened the door. I was older then and asked her what was wrong. She looked at me as if she had been hiding a big secret. "Before we adopted you, we had heard about your mother. She had disappeared and word was that she never wanted you. I had just wanted a baby, and I had felt guilty for taking you. I always' felt like God was punishing me for adopting you after the mother had ended hers tragically. We had changed it to a closed adoption to kept her from bothering us. I sometimes wonder if we had just left it alone would she still be alive today? I wanted to be a mother so badly that I always felt selfish for needing you to save me." I sat by my mother in shock at what she had just told me. "But when I found you all that guilt that I held went away and I was so terrified that I would never be the mother you wanted me to be. It didn't matter after all that you weren't my flesh and blood, what mattered was that we both had found a safe place to find our place in this world where we could find each other…"

That day, my mother had taught me that we shouldn't always try to look between the lines even if life can seem out of focus. No matter how hard we want to see the clear picture ahead of us; we don't' need to find reasons in the disorder. But why do we still question every choice we make? Even after the matter? Yet sometimes we want to go back and hesitate as if we aren't sure. John Milton used it in the book Paradise Lost "With Heavens ray and tempered, they shoot forth so beauteous, opening to the ambient light?" The answer is so simple. As humans we want life to be ambient, so we can feel safe; maybe it's the only way out of uncertainty…

9

Chapter Fifteen
(Patty)

"Hi," I try to be polite and cheery. "Chai latte please." I am at Marcella's coffee shop again. As I look around there is a different man at the register. As I lean up front, I feel stupid but ask "Could you tell me if Luke Bolan is working today?" There is a long line behind me and I feel rushed as someone behind me complains.

"Just a minute." He goes in the back and comes out with another older lady who stares at me as if I'm crazy.

"Mrs. Marcella Bolan, his wife, died months ago. Were you looking for her?" The old woman looks nervous at me as she wipes her hands on her apron. After explaining to her the details, about how I had just spoken with Luke days ago, she finally stops me and explains that Luke Bolan had only worked here back in 1989, but tragically died in 1992, nineteen years ago.

Before she can finish, I step back in shock. "What? but I just saw him…" I suddenly feel sick as I my head starts to throb again. Was it true? Why hadn't I heard about this? What had happened? Had my concussion caused me to forget?

"I'm so sorry." She tells me.

I sit down with my drink and stare out the window. I am shaking and feel angry as I look down at my chai latte now getting cold. I notice the man in the table sitting across from me.

He is dressed in a cassock black robe with a golden cross necklace hanging around his neck. He must have heard the conversation and turns around.

"I'm sorry, did you know Luke Bolan?" he asks.

I look up and wipe my eyes. "Yes, we had been childhood friends, when I had lived in Providence, we were neighbors. Do you know what happened? Was it his heart?" I take a sip of my chai and sadly listen to him introduce himself as Father David the priest from St Mary's down the street.

"Well, didn't you read it in the papers? Luke died in the 1992 fire at St Lindon's church. He was coming out of the gas station when we saw Father Eugene trapped inside. I was there when it happened, and pulled him out from under the roof that had caved in. They were not able to save him at the hospital. I think they told me the carbon monoxide had weakened his heart." He paused and cleared his throat.

That's' strange I think, I guess I had forgotten. "I have been suffering from amnesia from a car accident and hoping to recover." I tell him. "But I just bought that church, it's mine now." I tell him.

"Oh?" He looks over at me curiously.

I suddenly feel sad as the feeling in my stomach turns sour. "Well, was there a funeral?"

He looks up at me sadly. "Yes, it was big, the whole town knew he was a hero for what he did." "I'm sorry, what is your name?" "Patty." I tell him.

He looks nervously at his watch. "Well, I need to go, but I would like to see that new remodeled church of yours. If you want to talk sometime, here is my card."

As I drive back home, I try to think about where I was back in 1992. I had just finished art school and moved back home to Kentucky. I had been with the same boyfriend for two years but we had just broken up. It was at a time I had been struggling in life and had wanted to give up. I really felt disconcerted. Maybe that was why I had been so depressed. Had I suppressed the shock of my friend's death also? I needed to talk to that priest, he had told me he had been there when Luke had died. I didn't know what was wrong with me. Was that why I was seeing and hearing things? My doctor had prescribed medication for my grief but I didn't think it would give me hallucinations.

This town of Waynesville like any small town, was a place that had a past. It had been founded in 1797. Old or young everyone here seemed to have a story about its' history. As I drive on the small two -lane road back home, I pass old antique shops and wonder why do people give away their most precious values? Why do we want to get rid of those objects that share so many stories handed down from generation to generation? Is there such value in keeping those things that once held purpose?

My adoptive mother had reminded me, "to never forget who I was because being adopted didn't define me." She wanted me to believe that I was loved. That my past was not defined by who I came from. However, all along I felt as if I was some piece of old furniture waiting to be sold at a dime store. I knew that no matter how much people on the outside ripped open my vulnerable heart, I had a God who loved me and protected me from the doubt that sometimes took away my strength. If I believed that my circumstances could never be changed, I could allow myself to face those things that had hurt me, and then let go of my expectations of it. That's why memories are the key to everything they unlock the doors that we kept shut. However, just because we don't remember something doesn't mean the memory is invaluable.

When I was about ten a kitten appeared on our doorstep one day. I didn't understand that it might belong to someone. I loved cats, and had always wanted one, but my dad was allergic.

I didn't care, the kitten was a beautiful calico and it had come to me hungry and scared. Excited about my new pet, shutting our metal fence, I trapping it inside our backyard. It seemed needy with its fur tattered, as it cried wanting me to hold it. I did not tell my parents at first what I had found. However, I thought I could keep it a secret for longer. When the kitten had tried to get out, it couldn't climb over the fence. Instead, it had tried to make its way through the small openings in the chain-like fence. The next morning when I went to check on it, I saw that the kitten had gotten halfway through the hole, until its head had gotten stuck as it tried to get out to the other side. It would have died of strangulation, if I hadn't admitted the situation to my father. He quickly grabbed his plyers and had to break the fence wire as we tried to pry the poor kitten out. By then, the fur around its neck had turned pink and bloody, from where it had pulled and struggled to get out.

We soon found out that it had belonged to the mean old lady next door, whose outdoor cat just had kittens. She had never liked me, and likewise would never let me pet her cats. The kitten had survived, but it would have that scar around its neck forever. I cried because I hadn't realized that I had hurt it. The poor kitten just wanted to go back home to its mother. The fact that it didn't need me left me horrified. My dad was not mad at me, but I will never forget what he told me "Sometimes, you have to let go of the things that you think you want; you can't keep everything that you think is yours."

I had wanted to save my husband, because that was what I was supposed to do. He was just like that little kitten who had trusted in me. I had thought they could fix him, and I thought God would give him back to me. But that black shadow of doubt, kept whispering its negative thoughts into my ears. I couldn't do a single thing about it. Every part of you wants to do something to change it, but in reality, there's nothing you can do. The fact was, Phillip's destiny wasn't mine to decide it was God's. I might have had to decide in making the choice to let them turn off those machines. Putting myself at someone else's fate, it is hard to put your faith in something you cannot see. I wanted to pretend that I could do this on my own, but the reality was I didn't have to.

I didn't like the idea that the past can create an illusion that things were better and happier, but it can also weaken you making you stuck in your memories of failed expectations and disappointments. It holds you back from finding more happiness in life. If there was another thing I had learned, it was that change, disappointments, or circumstances, don't control us. It's only how we react to them. We can let disappointment hurt us, or we can turn them into something beautiful. It's not up to us to carry so much sorrow when all along God is there to take our pain and to hear are cries. It might be impossible to believe at first, but sometimes those tragedies can be the best thing that ever happens to us.

Chapter Sixteen
(David)

David remembered the first time he and his mother had come to the St Lindon's Catholic church; it was Father Eugene that had come up to them to introduce himself. He had just been a young boy as he looked up at the high ceiling and stained-glass windows. But there was something about that church, not just because Father Eugene had seemed authoritive but he always felt as if something had been watching him. He didn't know what it was, but it made him feel anxious. He had tried to suppress it inside him, but it kept coming back to the surface. The only way for him to understand was to pretend it was all just a theory, in his mind he had tried to pretend that evil did not exist. However, he couldn't ignore those piercing blue eyes Father Eugene had staring down at him in the pew. In Catholic school he was taught again and again that God was everywhere watching everything you do but the devil was real. "Evil is all around us, it romes freely, the devil doesn't hide." he was taught

He had remembered the message one day; Father Eugene had trembled as he shouted. "We are free to make our own choices, good and evil are not absolute, but when we do terrible things, confession is not enough. It's up to us to understand in forgiveness. In return Jesus forgave us even though death is our punishment."

David thought of the day of his father's funeral he was twenty-three and too old to cry in front of anyone. His mother looked over and put her arms around him. His father had died in Vietnam and he was angry and confused. It was the last letter that his father had sent them that had made him upset the most. In the letter he had tried to explain why he couldn't fight his enemy without surrender. All he had wanted was peace and not war. To him death was not the enemy but the only way for him to end his part in peace. In the last sentence he had written: "We think we have free will, but we don't; rather we have no free will in what we do because there is sin and sins have consequences. There is a war within each of us. The only way to overcome our weaknesses, is to not hide from that darkness that might conquer you, but to face and surrender to what might overtake us. In the end it's your choice to face whatever could destroy you." He knew his father's last words were only for his troubled son...

David turned the key to the door and walked inside the old bedroom his mother had stayed in. The room even smelled of her lilac powder she had always worn. He wasn't sure why he had kept all her clothes and he couldn't remember what box he had put them in. He had been so frustrated with the whole deal. He hadn't wanted to pack away all her China, old jazz records handed down from her grandfather, and tarnished jewelry from her sister. He had stuffed them into salvation boxes to give away. The fact was, this room had sat just like this for decades after she had died, and he never had cleaned it out. He felt it was time to stop putting it off.

He remembered when he had gotten the phone call that day, it was a year after Mary had died. His mother had wanted to meet him at a nearby diner. When she told him that she was given two months, she had asked him why God was punishing her when she thought she had done everything good in her life.

He told her that sickness was not from God, it was from sin, and sin is from the devil. "But I am afraid it's too late for me," she had told him. "I haven't forgiven myself for the transgressions I have committed." David was confused. "Please you can tell me, I will understand. If there is something else that happened that night or if you saw someone with Mary it's important that I know. God will forgive you."

His mother finally confessed. She looked at him with tears in her eyes as he held her hand. "I knew she was going to leave that night before she disappeared. I had found the train ticket earlier hidden in her room. She wouldn't tell me where she was going. So, I took my car and went to the train station. However, they had said she hadn't checked in. I had looked around and did not see her. It had been raining, it was dark out, and I had been angry at her again. On my way back, I crossed the bridge, driving fast I hit something on the road. When I got out of my car, I saw blood on the ground, and someone's rosary. When I went down under the bridge, I noticed the sweater was Mary's. I looked down at the lake below and realized that my car had hit someone. I saw the red sweater floating above the water and realized what I had done."

The sun was now coming through the windows and began to let a little light into the room. It created a shadow on one side of the wall. He had read somewhere that shadow and light never separate on their own; they are always together, visible, with the invisible. He knew the beauty of life was made up of light and shadows. What did it mean? A shadow is the absence of light when trying to pass through an object, it absorbs the light that is blocked. It creates a refraction; stopping its direction. No shadow can hide from the light that crested it. In the same way, he had known that evil is the absence of God. To measure the amount of dark you measure the amount of light. They cannot hide from each other. He had learned that sin is the result of what happens when man does not have Gods love in his heart. He knew that sometimes man's direction gets blocked but that didn't mean that one had to wait forever trying to focus on what he couldn't see. She had confessed to him that it was a hit and run. He had wished his mother could have admitted her own mistake to the authorities.

David opened his Bible. He liked to read his daily verse. This time it stuck to him like honey. "And God will wipe away every tear from their eyes. And death shall be no more. And neither mourning, nor crying out, nor grief shall be anymore. For the first things have passed away." Revelations 21:4. He squinted and dropped down to the eighth verse: "But the fearful, and unbelieving, and the abominable and murderers, and fornicators, and all liars, these shall be a part of the pool burning with fire and sulphur." He felt the tightness in his chest as he tried to choke back his grief.

As a Catholic priest his responsibilities had all started to fall under him decades ago after the old St Lindon church had caught fire. David had grown to follow the teachings from the Catholic seminary. He had followed all his sacrament's, he had studied his Bible, and he had prayed daily. Had he been hiding behind his religion all along, hoping it would be his safety net, redeeming him towards salvation, covering up his weaknesses? He had tried to become the hero when he wanted to save Luke and Father Eugene from the fire. He had hoped it would redeem him and save him from the town's accusations. He had tried so hard to put it all behind him.

Mary hadn't killed herself it had been an accident. No one knew the truth, because his mother never confessed. He was the only one who held her secret. Now he felt he had failed himself. Why did he always feel like he was the underdog? When he couldn't face his own narcistic ego? He had wanted to be the strong one in his mother's eyes. She taught him to say his prayers every night before he went to bed and she told him that there were angels watching over him. But she never warned him about the evil lurking around the corner; that ambivalence was real, and that he needed his armor of faith, to protect him from the doubts he held under his conscience.

David remembered how he had finally realized how much he let it poison him, making him rethink his choices. He had gone to Father Eugene and confessed that he had made a terrible mistake wanting to become a priest. "How can I give so much advice when I struggle with my own sins? I don't feel good enough. I could have saved my best friend." He had told him. Maybe it was his conscious always haunting him. He thought it would be easy and he wasn't good at commitments. "Please don't give up, in time you will grow and learn that no one is perfect." Father Eugene had told him. David knew that there was nothing he could have done to change what had happened that day but he always let it become his threshold. It seemed he could not be set free of his remorse, maybe he just needed to believe that a part of him still had lived...

Chapter Seventeen
(Patty)

Somedays, when I woke up in the mornings, I didn't get that feeling that you feel when you have something to look forward to that gets you out of bed. Like making pancakes for someone you love, or sitting outside watching the sun rise over the town. Instead, I prayed. I looked at that empty spot where Phillip should have been, and tried to think good thoughts. I didn't know how much time would pass before details would fade. I didn't know what I would remember from one day until the next. The sad reality was I no longer would feel those small moments like his funny laugh or his soft kisses that would leave me breathless. The truth is there is no secret way to let go of someone who is now gone. There is no recipe, formula, hypothesis, or medicine that can get rid of the sadness that we feel. That's when patience is a virtue and where God can give us the courage and strength to hold on.

When I lived in Providence, we had an old peach tree in our back yard. One day I asked my mother why it never grew peaches. She told me that it had to be pruned, that it would take time for the branches to grow into buds, and then the buds needed to be pollinated by the bees. As the buds grew and absorbed water it would grow into fruit. "Over time and as seasons pass it will draw nourishment from those surrounding it." she had promised. It seemed such a long process just to get a simple tree to bear fruit.

We had to wait a long time. "It just doesn't grow wild; nature has to tame it from the outside." she had said. "Or it won't give us the part of it that we want." Does that what it feels like when God is trying to show us that we need to be pruned? Why does it take us so long to bear fruit? Is it because we are drawing nourishment from the wrong source? Sometimes pruning thorns out of our life can be painful.

I think back again to a memory of something I will never forget. It was the last day me and Luke would see each other. I was eleven and he was thirteen. My dad took us through the drive through to get some ice cream at dairy queen, and then he had to stop at the store to get some milk. As he ran in, he left us alone to wait in the car. As we licked our chocolate cones, I remember how Luke sat in the back, as he sadly told me the reason why they were moving. His parents were getting a divorce. I turned around to question him, as his togue licked the melting ice cream. "But I promise I will see you again, and I will save up enough money so I can buy a fancy house right next to yours, and we can see each other every day." I worried as I looked over at him sitting in the back seat. I noticed that some of the ice cream had dripped onto the bottom of the white part of the seat that I was sitting in. I had wanted him to wipe it off, because my dad had warned us not to spill any. However, I looked at the stain that had dripped, unaware of Luke who kept talking. I didn't say anything though as I turned around. I hoped that it would forever mark that special moment between us.

The chocolate stain hidden behind the bottom of that seat was unnoticed by my parents for years, until my dad had to replace that old chevy station wagon. As years passed the brown stain grew hard and deep where it had settled into the fabric hidden by my parents. That mark had left behind a memory of my best friend. All along I had wanted it to be a reminder of hope. Sometimes when I looked at it, it seemed to fade under my tears. I had wanted it to stay there forever on that back seat. I had wanted it to remind me that I would go back to find him someday. I had to surrender to my expectation knowing that life always gives us second chances. I had believed all along in the future. However, I knew that whatever happened later down the road, I would learn to face those unpleasant circumstances that made its mark on me. Whether it be a broken heart, a death of a loved one, or a lost toy. I would run my fingers gently over that hard-sticky stain over and over. Someday I would fall in love and lose them and find new friends and lose them again. I had wondered why do good things sometimes get ignored, but the things that disappoint you in life, like those stains that are left behind, why does it never fade away?

After a long day of unpacking my boxes, I find the old newspapers about the fire of the church the realtor had given me. It is labeled **"Fire of St Lindon's Church Questioned as Accident."** I had remembered hearing about it from my mother back when I had been away at art school. She had told me that two people had died and one of them had been Father Eugene.

The first article I see is labeled from April 1992. It describes how the fire arsons tried to investigate the problem. They had thought the cause was from a blown fuse or a faulty gas line. They had looked for an ignition source or a fuel source but neither could be found. They had only come up with proof that it was an accident but due to the low burning point, unusual burn patterns on the walls of the church, and high heat stress there was no evidence that someone else had started it. The mass candles had probably been knocked over and it had gone up into the curtains towards the ceiling. The fire department could not find why Father Eugene hadn't seen the smoke sooner. The fire seemed to have spread up to the ceiling causing the roof to burn first and collapse. Father Eugene had been down the basement in his office with the door shut and possibly had fallen asleep. By the time he awoke it was too late and the man who tried to rescue him had already suffered when the roof collapsed on them.

As I flip through the other papers from April 9th, I notice the headlines in boldface:

1992 Mysterious Stranger Goes Inside Burning Church.

"A local member of St Lindon's Catholic church risked his life yesterday after what witnesses described him as heroic. The young man was identified as thirty-two -year- old Luke Bolan from Waynesville, Ohio. He had been at the gas station around nine pm when he saw the smoke coming from the building. Running towards the church he went inside to save Father Eugene trying to open the windows. By the time the medics and fire department had arrived the young man was seen unconscious along with Father Eugene outside the building. A witness on the scene had pulled the men out and had tried to revive one of them. Both were badly injured and taken to Memorial hospital. The fire was quickly attended to and the St Lindon's church was not destroyed. Father Eugene aged fifty-four the priest of the church, had sustained injuries to the head but medics were not able to save him. The other man who was identified as Luke Bolan, was taken to the emergency room where he was unconscious but died two days later of heart complications. This terrible tragedy has affected all of us in the town of Waynesville. We will miss the brave men who died in this unpredictable accident. The St Lindon's church will remain closed until the damage can be cleared up and until further notifications have been posted."

The Luke I had known had been a hero after all. The fire trucks couldn't get there in time, and he had no other choice. He knew he just couldn't let an innocent life end. The Luke I had known would have done anything to save anyone. He had such a big heart that not even I could understand his passion. I dig further down to see if there is a clipping of an obituary but there is none. I would have to go to the library to find it.

The doctors told me my medication could cause me to confuse what was not real and that sometimes grief could mess up my perception of reality. I should have realized that there was something about the way Luke had appeared and disappeared to me at the coffee shop. I close my eyes and try to breathe. In my younger days I had learned to rely on meditation to clear my mind. But this had to stop I didn't want to see people who weren't there. Then I thought of something, Father David had told me that he had believed in angels. Had Luke come to me because he wanted to reassure me, that he was, okay? Did I believe in what I saw? The reality began to impose on me the way a transparency does over a page, maybe all along I just needed to believe it was true, that angels could be real. Did I believe it had taken my pain?

Chapter Eighteen
(David)

David was planning on taking a trip to Providence, Kentucky next month and start the long search for his daughter. Time was running out and he did not want to put it off any longer. During his operation of receiving a new lung he thought of all the things he had wished he had done. He kept thinking that he had waited too long. However, just last month during his checkup, they had told him the cancer had spread to his liver and colon. The new lung would only give him a little more time. He wanted to find out who the person was that had donated their lung to him. It was important, but he was still waiting on the letter from the hospital.

As decades went by and the damage was replaced inside St Lindon's church people began to witness something haunting it. He remembered how there were reports that someone had seen a young woman looking out from the top windows. Another walking by had witnessed seeing a priest standing outside the back praying. The police had been called numerous times about the gas stove that kept turning on and setting off the fire alarm. Lights in the church began turning on and off when it was empty. However, they just had thought it was something crawling over the switches or some other bad rewiring explaining it. He wondered if it had anything to do with the same shadow, he saw in the window that night of the fire. The ghost like image had faded so quickly but he had thought it just his imagination.

David remembered the day of the funeral. He was in charge of the eulogy. "Luke Bolan had been a good man who had died saving another, he will be remembered as a husband, friend, and hero." When he couldn't finish, he had broken down. "He had died in my arms… but sometimes we can't save those whom we think need saving." He remembered looking into the crowd then at Luke's wife Marcella whom had been so upset. Then he saw Luke's mother come up to take over for him. When he looked ahead, he thought he saw someone in the back window look into the church. The person had looked just like Mary. It had just been for a moment but she had appeared to him wearing the red sweater she always wore. When David walked off the stage he couldn't focus. He had thought he was going crazy. He had felt so tired but didn't tell anyone what he saw. He walked out the back door and looked towards the horizon. In the sky was a beautiful double rainbow. It stretched up towards the sky and over the church. He remembered looking at it as if God wanted to tell him something. He knew it was God's promise of faithfulness.

The funeral was big and the whole town had come for the ceremony. They buried Luke next to his father. Father Eugene had wanted to be cremated, so they just said a couple of words, and spread out his ashes over the back of the church. It was very rainy that day and he remembered how gloomy and sad it had been. The wetness had soaked through his black dress shoes. The cold chill had crept into his bones. He remembered watching a silly dove perch on a tree next to them. It wouldn't stop singing as if it knew what was going on. He remembered how Marcella; Luke's wife had come up to him. "You are a hero too; you had tried to help them both. God will bless you in Heaven." He was angry at first about the accident, blaming Father Eugene over some careless candles. This time he needed to ask for God's forgiveness, for not understanding.

David parked his truck in the old parking lot. He got out and stood at the doorway. He looked up at the old St Lindon's Catholic church, it still looked the same. The roof from the outside held marks from the fire, the new shingles didn't match the old wood. Yet he would have never guessed that it had once almost been destroyed. He looked at the doors as his stomach quenched, and he suddenly felt nervous. He rang the doorbell as he heard the chimes from inside. There was a rustle as the door opened.

"Hello how are you?" he looked down at the lady who reminded him so much of Mary.

"Yes, Father, I was just baking some snickerdoodle cookies. Would you like to come in?"

He paused before stepping in as if he didn't want to remember the old church. The woman Patty looked up at him. David noticed the same familiar green eyes behind the glasses and dark greyed hair. She was small in height like Mary and looked to be in her late forties. Maybe he was imagining things but there was something familiar about the way she spoke. She seemed grateful to see him. He had given her his card that day in the coffee shop. He really had wanted to see this place for himself, but he felt like he was moving slowly as if in some strange lucid dream. He had wanted to face the fact that this church still held its ground.

It was nearing the end of July and outside the weather was humid. However, the cold chill would not leave his bones as he stepped inside and looked around and up at the high vaulted ceiling. He noticed the black suet still on the uppermost part of the wood; the part that had been saved. Inside the light shown from the tall stained -glass windows. It gave a spectrum of reds yellows and blues over the whole hallway as if it was meant to cover up the imperfections. It felt welcoming as he once had remembered it. David tried to not choke back his thoughts as he once remembered the men who had died inside that day.

"So why did you come here to Waynesville? Was it just to buy this church and find Luke?" he asked her.

"Oh, I just needed to come back and start over."

She led him in as he followed her to the kitchen. David looked around and then looked down. Something brushed against his leg. "Hello there. And who's this?" He looked at the calico cat that seemed friendly at first.

"That's Ramona." She usually doesn't like strangers but I guess she likes you." The cat eyed him and sniffed the hand that gently reached down to pet its head. Patty had just lost someone dear to her, and he knew what that felt like too. "Well, I'm sorry about your friend Luke."

She sat down in front of him and sat back. "To be honest, I was left here as a baby in 1962; my mother dropped me here in desperation. I was told Father Eugene had found me afterwards. I was that abandoned church baby you might have heard the story back then? My mother was the girl they found dead in the lake. So did you know Father Eugene or did you ever attend this church?"

"Yes, I did as a young boy and I knew Father Eugene pretty well. I remember that day they found you." David's neck turned red as he realized who she was. He sat down and started feeling dizzy. He wanted to tell her that she wasn't left and abandoned on purpose. It would explain why he felt so close to this stranger whom he had just met days ago.

"I'm sorry, Father are you feeling alright? I have cookies coming out soon." she told him. He nodded as she cleared the stack of papers piled on the table. "I'll get you some water." He watched her as she grabbed a glass and poured the water from a filter on the sink.

"Father, I asked you to come here for a reason. I was wondering if you knew anything about my mother when she had attended back then?"

David loosened his shirt as he tried to find the right words. "Yes, Mary was in my Sunday school class. She had known my mother well. Mary was a troubled girl, and had been in recovery from using. She had lived with my mother for a while, and we had tried to get her the help she needed. It was terrible when we heard the news that the body had been recovered from the lake."

"Do you think she had wanted a second chance when the open adoption was closed?" Patty asked him.

"Well, I'm not sure. I know the family had wanted to press charges for leaving you at that church. But she did come to me that week before she had disappeared."

"What?" Patty looked over at him with an accusing look.

"Yes, she had wanted to go to Providence to look for you. There had been some misunderstanding between her and my mother. She had gotten a bus ticket but she was told that she would have to leave the family alone who had authority over you. She came to me feeling sorrowful that she had messed everything up. If only I had called the police maybe it wouldn't have happened. Didn't your parents tell you about it from the newspapers?"

Patty looked at him with a questionable look on her face. "No, they didn't tell me the whole story. I suppose it was kept from me like some secret. However, I told them I didn't want to know the real story."

"I'm so sorry, I wished that they hadn't kept it from you." He told her.

She soon brought out a pan of fresh cookies and was putting them on a plate. The smell of spiced cinnamon made his stomach growl. "Well, that certainly is a story. Do you know who the father might have been? She asked him. David stared at the cookies. "I'm not sure, no one knew who it was."

He tried to smile as she kept talking about why she kept putting it off to come back and search for answers. He looked at her features, the dark wavy hair now grayed with age and her piercing green eyes behind her bifocals, she was a perfect match to Mary. He couldn't help but stare at her again wondering if he had just been dreaming. "Father David, how long has it been since you've come back here?"

"It's been about nineteen years since; I thought they would turn this church into a museum, a funeral home or something else. Maybe, someday, right?"

Patty looked at him and grinned. "Yes, this church could hold possibilities."

"We have you to thank for believing in it once again, it looks wonderful, and you did it all yourself. I'm sure people in town would enjoy seeing it once again."

Patty looked at him and bit into a cookie. "Yes, some things need fixing, but in time I think I can make it work. But I'm not going to turn it back into a church. How was Mary's funeral?" she asked him.

"Well, it was sudden. I don't remember it much myself but she was well remembered. You can go down to the Caesar creek cemetery and see where she was buried. It is a nice tombstone they had made it special for her." He ignored the cookies as he explained. "She was a good Christian, she just had problems." He noticed the small scar on Patty's forehead and remembered the car accident she had told him about and how her husband had died. He suddenly felt a deep empathy for her and was wondering how she was holding up. He felt like deflecting the subject. "I hope you are doing okay from your accident. PTSD is common after these situations. Sometimes the grief can make you go crazy."

"I'm doing okay, but I think I am seeing and hearing things in this place. Doors opening and shutting, and when I'm sleeping at night, I hear something in the basement coming from that office." She exclaimed.

"Oh, like what?" he leaned forward. He had wondered if she had seen the same ghostly figure in white as he had.

"I'm not sure. Why is that office room boarded and locked up downstairs? I need to see what's making all the noise in the basement. Could it be the old pipes behind the walls?"

David thought for a moment. "Oh, I think that room once was Father Eugene's office. However, I'm not sure why they would lock it. Maybe you should have it looked at by a professional."

"Father do you believe in angels?"

"Well maybe… tell me what do you believe?" She looked away and then out the window.

"I don't know. I was always taught as a Christian and believing in God that they were real. But I saw something it seemed so real and spoke to me."

"Who, your husband?"

"No, Luke." David sat up in his chair and felt dizzy.

"I thought it was the medication or the grieving of my husband but I'm not sure because it comes and goes. I've never experienced anything like this before. I saw Luke at the coffee shop and then he disappeared as if he came out from behind the walls. Then I heard someone in my basement the other day, I know I'm not crazy. At first, I thought it was someone breaking in but I keep the doors locked. It was coming from that priest's office as if there's something behind the door. At first, I thought it was my cat, but she never goes down there because she doesn't like stairs. I wasn't scared, I know Luke is gone, but why did I have this experience? Do you think it was his angel?"

"When you were at the coffee shop what did he tell you?"

"I just asked him about his wife Marcella, I guess she died of breast cancer. Do you know if that's true?"

David tried to find a logical reason. "Well, yes she died a couple months ago."

"I explained to him about my accident, and how Phillip died and told him how I had felt guilty about it. Then he disappeared, I thought I had just made him upset."

"Sometimes grief can do this to our minds. I know you are dealing with your memory loss but you might see people from your past or remember things you have repressed. I myself have been through similar loses but I can't explain why we can't separate reality from imagination, it's our minds way of dealing with the pain I guess." He took a sip of the water she had given him.

"On the other hand, I have never seen an angel, but maybe God has his ways of speaking to us through visions or dreams."

She seemed to watch him as if taking in every word. On the other hand, maybe she understood what it was like to try to trust someone with your memory. "It's okay." He told her. "I don't think you are crazy." He didn't like trying to rationalize his own thoughts and ideas. "I don't know why it's so hard to let it go." He finally explained, "but that's why God helps us through those difficult times. It's also important to have people you trust whom you can talk to."

The tears came as she started to sob. "My husband was my best friend, we spent eighteen years together. Why does God take away what we love the most?" She finally choked back the tears as she wiped her eyes. David struggled with the same question but he didn't have an answer. He sat and listened as she grabbed the tissues. "I will never be able to move on." She admitted. They were similar in so many ways. They both were blaming themselves for the guilt they had felt.

"I remember when I was eleven and Luke moved away, and how I wished that someone else would just move into that empty house. But it sat there for years empty and abandoned. I would walk by it and sometimes ring the doorbell to see if anyone had moved there yet. It was hard when my best friend had moved away, it was as if he had already died." Patty looked over at him. "I'm so sorry that I didn't come to the funeral."

David looked into her sad eyes that hid behind her greyed hair and the bifocals that framed her small features. Was she still repressing the guilt she couldn't face? Somehow, he couldn't find the reason as to why he was sitting in front of this woman he had only met days ago. Now he was sitting inside this church once again finding out that she had needed him all along when he thought she wouldn't. The reality was she was drawn to this church just as much as he was because it held a part of his past too. He was glad he could give her some information about Mary, Luke, and Father Eugene, it would help her find peace. He wanted to tell her who he was but he wasn't ready yet. The sad news was he was dying and there wasn't much time. He didn't want to stress her anymore.

"It wasn't your fault." He tried to encourage her, "but you can't run away from what you have lost, you must face it. Sometimes these things just happen but it's not up to us to figure it out. In time you will learn to forgive yourself."

David followed Patty as she showed him around the newly furnished church. He still was recovering from his operation and had to walk slowly. "I'm so grateful that you found a doner." she had told him, "It's good that people want to donate organs and save lives. I guess my view of that changed after my husband died. It really does make a difference if you give someone another chance."

David looked at the high vaulted ceiling made of wood. He remembered the long sanctuary where the pews sat before the alter and the stand Father Eugene had stood so high up on. He thought of the last time he had seen Mary sitting in the pew. Now it was a large hall where Patty used as an art gallery. It looked like she was an artist, she had many paintings hung on the walls. He looked around and walked up to one and stared up at it. It was a disfigured picture of a woman with dark hair in a red sweater standing in a corn field. The body was facing away towards the sky looking ahead towards a church. The picture hadn't much color, it mostly was greys, blues, and blacks. He looked over at it carefully. "That's' a recent one I had just finished." She told him. David had thought the woman Patty had painted had looked just like Mary. He remembered the red sweater the same one Patty had been wrapped up in as a baby. "Have you seen that red sweater before?" he asked her.

"No, I don't think they kept it, but I remember it from the photographs. She told him. David looked at the picture again maybe it was her looking towards the church because she was looking for that hope.

"I want to find more information about my mother who had died. I hope that the police office will have some kind of information or old newspapers. I guess the loss of my husband has brought me to this point. I didn't think I would care about coming back here to face all this. I just needed closure and to find people like friends who had known her."

"Well, we all have to learn how to deal with our past, even if it means digging up things we don't want to face." Patty looked up at him and nodded. David looked around and tried to bite his lip. "Yes, don't let it bother you. I am sure you will get through this. I am so glad we have gotten to meet and talk. But I will pray for your healing in dealing with those you have lost. Patty if you are suffering from a lot of anxiety, I would advise you to find someone like a specialist to talk through this."

He took her hand and prayed a quick prayer of peace and protection for her. However, he felt uneasy because he needed to tell her more. He knew she would find out from asking around town that he and Mary had been close. When she was ready, he would tell her that he was her father. "Keep in touch and let me know how you are doing." He told her. As she waved goodbye and closed the door behind him, he had the sense that someone was watching him. It was almost sundown as he put the key into his locked car and he looked behind him again. Up on the second story- stained glass window he thought he saw something move behind it. He squinted under the sun to get a better view. Ever so briefly it moved back behind the shadows...

Chapter Nineteen
(Patty)

"Everything okay down there?" I called from the stairs. The plumber is in my house trying to fix my hot water heater. It is soon too quiet again and as I scramble my slippers on, I walk down the steep stairway to see what is going on. "Well, did you find the problem?" he doesn't answer me, instead he is standing in front of the boarded- up room with his back towards me as if he has blacked out. "Sir?" he doesn't move as I wonder what is going on. It is dark and I beam my flashlight at the closed door what was he staring at?

This time I am convinced that I am not imagining things. Suddenly I hear something like buzzing flies coming from the priest's office across the room. I blink my eyes and direct my flashlight and turn towards it. My heart begins to pound so loud that I could hear it inside my chest. The noise seems to get louder and louder as it surrounds us. "What the?" I look over and notice that the room has changed I am no longer in a basement. Suddenly, I see a large animal- like being come out from behind the boarded- up door in the form of something beautiful. It was so magnificent yet threatening, I step back afraid. It comes towards me as its bright glow surrounds me blinding my eyes. I try to look away and cover my face but I want to see it. I hear its winged movement come towards me in slow motions. As I open my eyes, I see that it is not Luke but a man. As he reaches out his hand and touches my forehead, I try to step back. "Don't be afraid." It tells me. I am mesmerized by its magnificence. Then suddenly the voice speaks directly at me. "You have suffered a loss, let me take all your pain." "Who are you?" I question it. I see that it has come towards me, with its arms out, waiting as if wanting me to surrender to it. "I'm sorry, but I can't." I cry, "God can take all your pain, you do not have to carry your burdens all alone." Suddenly I feel warm as I take its hand and cry out in grief. "I miss Phillip so much." Then I see it fade away as it goes back behind the wall and I am in the dark basement again.

"Hey, what's that?" I hear the plumber come back to himself. He has no idea what had just happened. The sound of the buzzing noise in my head has disappeared. "Wow those are some noisy old pipes behind that room." He questions. He tries to turn the door handle but it is locked. "We will get someone to come out soon to fix this." He exclaims. I am so tired and disoriented as we walk back up the stairs.

As I sit down in my kitchen chair, I notice that I'm covered in black suet. The plumber doesn't notice and looks over at me suspiciously. I swallow to catch my breath. My doctor had warned me that I might suffer from PTSD and I realize now that I think this is true. However, if I had encountered an angel, somehow I did feel better. "But, I don't see any evidence of racoons in your basement." He rambles on. He politely explains that he thought the problem seemed to be coming from something behind that room. He makes an appointment for someone to come over to break down the door and look around. "Lady this place gives me the creeps." He tells me as I closed the door. I look at my receipt he has just given me and notice something strange, it's copied from my maiden's name.

I wanted to believe that there are a few chances between this life and the next where something extraordinary can happen where something like this just happens. Had I seen an angel? Was this really happening to me?

I am in my basement getting out the boxes again. It is four in the afternoon, and I sit down in my kitchen to dig for the realtor's papers. I wanted to find out what had happened to this church after it had gone up for sale.

I flip ahead to another folder describing how they tried to sell the church over the nineteen years it was abandoned. Relators had claimed that they had heard something coming from the strange room boarded up in the basement. At night neighbors who walked by kept reporting seeing a young girl looking out from the window. Even the contractors who had tried to fix the damaged roof, had claimed that something did not want them there when their ladder was suddenly knocked over. The church was taken off the market again when the realtor had to close it due to its reputation. Luckily, some donations went forward to keep paying its property fees. The place stood empty for decades, and people in town wondered if it just needed to be turned it into something else.

Maybe, I wanted to believe that my heartache could be healed, challenging me to look inward. Maybe, what I was going through, was no different than trying to understand why we sometimes need to face our worst fears. I learned a long time ago to stop expecting everything to stay the same. It was something I had read in a book. "A denied expectation hurts more than a denied hope. While a fulfilled hope makes us happier than a fulfilled expectation."

I remembered a day when Luke was about eleven and had wanted me to jump off the diving board at the local pool. He was not afraid to do it so why couldn't I? He had me on a string, like a puppet waiting for a show. I wanted so much to make him like me. It is difficult pretending to be flawless when you aren't. I worried that If I didn't do it, I would let him down. He expected me to do it and I wanted to give him that hope.

I climbed that ladder with fifteen steps and looked down at the deep end wondering what was going to happen to me. I hadn't told him that I didn't know how to swim but I convinced myself that I could do it. When Luke had bet his buddies that I was going to jump, I couldn't let him down. When I jumped into the water, I didn't realize how deep under gravity could pull me. Trying to swim upwards I tried to hold my breath and made my way up. Once above water, I paddled too much, splashing water into my face and choking on it. Getting water into my throat I tried to make my way to the low end. "Help!" I cried.

Luckily the lifeguard came after me, and asked me if I was okay. That moment I had felt stupid. I couldn't look at my friend because I was ashamed. I had almost drowned and now I had to face my punishment, I had lied. "I'm sorry I just wanted you to see that I could do it by myself." I told him. I hadn't realized how he perceived me afterwards. "You shouldn't have done it unless you were ready. If you were just thinking of yourself then I could have helped you learn to swim." I close my eyes and wonder after all these years; I shouldn't have done it. I should have waited until I had learned to swim. I had wanted to jump because I wanted to prove to him that I could face my own battles on my own. Sometimes we need to realize that we can't do everything on our own. It's okay to ask for help instead of pretending you can handle it on your own.

I thought I was the only one who had trouble when it seems you have no other choice, but to cross that line, when you want to try to look good so you don't feel insecure. The fact was I felt silly every time I failed at something. On the other hand, it is more important to try to face the fact instead of burying yourself behind your uncertainty. You grow up drowning in your own insecurities and wonder who will rescue you. Sometimes you don't look for the answer that could save you. All along I had been lying to myself, trying to cover up what I didn't know. Asking for God's help is not a weakness, sometimes He is the only one who can take your hand, and teach you how to swim.

§

Chapter Twenty
(David)

David went into his house, grabbed a flashlight, and then he went upstairs. He had not been down to the cemetery since last week when he had visited Mary's grave. Upstairs he opened the old room and reached into the top dresser drawer. He knew it was in there somewhere, under his mother's Bible, he wanted to find the rosary that had belonged to Mary. His mother had kept it over the years when the investigators told her they didn't need it. It was a reminder to not forgot who she was. He shoved his hand towards the back and felt the small object between his fingers. He grabbed it and looked at the shiny cross at the end. Was it his imagination, or did it look different? He looked at it again. He wasn't sure because he had never paid much attention to it before. He rubbed his fingers over the shiny silver beads. His mother had carried it around with her always, until she had put it away in a safe place. He never understood the meaning of why anyone would need to carry such a simple piece of jewelry for protection. His mother had warned him that it helped her with each prayer of faith, as each bead had represented a certain apostle's creed.

That's how David learned to follow his Sacrament's and do his confession when he could. He knew that his mother had always prayed for his peacefulness, but maybe she had been praying for herself to move on so she could forgive herself.

He took the rosary and shoved it into his pocket. It reminded him of something from long ago. He remembered when his mother had told him that she didn't want to tell the police where she was that night. Why had she wanted to lie? It had been several weeks after the body was found the investigators started to suspect that David and his mother were withholding evidence but nothing could be proved. He could only think that maybe his mother had been angry at Mary for abandoning her problems after she had tried so hard to help her. Likewise, Mary took her grandchild away from the family who loved and wanted to help her. Maybe his mother all along had just snapped.

David pulled into the side street facing the cemetery and grabbed the white carnations he had picked up. He slowly got out and suddenly he felt sad. "Can one be forgiven if he can't help thinking horrible things?" it was one of the questions that his congregation had asked him. Sometimes he had no answers. "We've all done things that we regret sometimes." He had told them. However, maybe he should have realized that these were questions he should have asked himself, since all along he was the one with all the secrets ...

David soon found the graves next to each other. He laid the flowers on his mother Sarah's tombstone and his father's next to it. He couldn't help but hold back his tears. He stooped down to brush off the dead grass around the graves. He missed his father to, they had spent so little time together before he had left for the war. He was glad that he had someone who had really loved him, at least for a short while. He wished that he hadn't made the same mistake of not being able to be there for his child. When he thought of his mother, she had felt so alone dealing with the loss it made him realize how much it had torn them apart.

As a young boy, after his father had died, David would sometimes wake up fearful in the middle of the night, convinced that something evil was waiting for him under his bed. It would make a constant scratch under the floorboards as if wanting to be found out. He then would shove the covers over his head, close his eyes tightly until his angry thoughts went away. He felt the monster was watching, trying to provoke him, as if it wanted to hurt him. Every night he got down on his knees, and he did the sign of the cross before he went to bed. Then he put his rosary, under his pillow. It was the only way he felt protected from the fearful thoughts that crept into his mind. He was too proud to cry for his mother to comfort him. In the same way, he wanted her to believe that he was strong on his own, because that's when he knew that monsters could be real.

It was getting dark at the cemetery as David turned his flashlight on. He prayed a quick prayer "Please God if you can hear me, help me face this so I can find peace." He was reminded of Psalms 121; "I will lift my eyes to the hills where does my help come from? My help comes from the Lord, the Maker of heaven and earth." David had struggled to accept that he had suffered under others mistakes. He should have asked for God's help when he felt lost.

David walked over to Mary's small tombstone. He laid the flowers on it. Today, he was the only one in the cemetery. He read the Bible verse they had inscribed on the front. "I go and prepare a place for you, and I will come again, and I will take you to myself so that where I am there you will also be." He had hoped Mary was at peace in Heaven. He knew how she had died but to him she had been a hero. He wanted to erase the lies the town had believed in but he had wanted to protect his mother and his reputation. Back then he realized his selfish mistake but it was too late to fix it.

He was about to turn around when he heard something from behind him. He looked around, to see who else was there, but he knew was the only one in the cemetery. Maybe it was just an animal he thought. If there were mischief kids in the area, he was hoping that they weren't after those flowers he had just put on the tombstones. He didn't think being out here alone at the gravesite would bother him, but he was feeling anxious again. The voices came at him as if mocking him. Was he just getting old? or maybe he was losing his mind.

Suddenly he heard something shout from behind him. "Repent!"

"Who's there?" he felt stupid talking to the darkness.

The voice was louder this time. "Confess!"

David started to walk faster towards his car. "What do you want? Who are you?" he shouted to the darkness.

He was so scared that he didn't see what had made him trip onto the ground. By the light of the street lamp, he didn't see anyone or anything. "You could have saved her." The voice whispered.

As he tried to get up something grabbed his leg. "What the...?" "Help!" he shouted. "Leave me alone!" the menacing laughter echoed into the silent night. David was shaking as he got up to dig for his car keys. He didn't look back as he ran towards his truck and jumped in. He pushed down on the gas, and wiped the sweat off his face as he drove back home. Why wouldn't his conscience leave him alone? As he quickly drove away and parked into his driveway, he realized that Mary's rosary necklace was no longer in his pocket. It had fallen out at the cemetery. He could not fight this any longer, it was quietly swallowing him up from somewhere so deep it felt unreachable...

The dream kept him this time. He was young again and he was driving towards the bridge. He hadn't much time but he was at the gas station. He opened up the love letter in his pocket. He was going to meet Mary at the church across the street. They were going to meet at the train station secretly after they were married. However, when he arrives at the church, he sees that it is on fire. Immediately stopping his car, he runs towards the building. Inside, behind the smoke was Mary looking out from behind the window. David can't get inside realizing that she is trapped. It was a silly dream but it had always' haunted him.

When David was a young deacon and altar boy, he had studied hard under Father Eugene's tutoring. He had performed the Eucharist at Mass while none of the other altar boys got the privilege. He had always known that Father Eugene would teach him and help him with his questions. They had once shared a close relationship where he would go to him for advice. "Guilt distinguishes us from God, but sin separates us from ourselves." He had told him one day.

After Mary's body had been found, David and Father Eugene had grown cold towards each other. He didn't like the town gossiping about them as to what they were keeping from the police. There was one small clue his mother had never realized when questioned by the police. Did she have any articles of clothing that had belonged to Mary? The dogs could sniff the material and then match it to the scent of where she might have gone. Sarah had given them the red sweater that Mary had left with David. When the dogs matched the scent to the bridge this gave them another reason to look in the lake. It was the only way to find her because she hadn't gotten onto the train.

That last day in hospice before his mother had breathed her last breath, she took his hand and wanted to ask him something. "Do you know why Mary was so upset that day?" she had asked him. He didn't need to say anything his face expression was louder than words. But he admitted; "I told her that I didn't need her in my life if she couldn't change." He wished all along that he had gone after her when she left the church that night. He knew she was going to the train station. If only he had gone after her than his mother wouldn't have hit her with his car. David had blamed himself for killing her too.

9

Chapter Twenty-One
(Patty)

This morning I am ready to go to the police station. I park at the parking lot and hesitate to get out of my truck. It had been so long ago; would they still have information about me, or her? "Hello." I tell the officer behind the window. "I would like to speak to an investigator."

A tall man comes out from behind the door. He introduces himself as officer Lawrence. I follow him into his office.

"And what is the reason or concern?" he looks down at me as I sit at the desk. "I would like some information about a case from the St Lindon church; it's about the girl Mary who abandoned her baby from 1962." He looks at me as if I have lost my mind.

"Ok Mrs...."?

"My name is Patty Wilkinson. I left a message a couple days ago?"

"Well, that case was a very long time ago, let me check in the files under the name. I remember it way back, but I think it was a suicide after the body was found." He types some information into a computer and coughs as he gets up to look through some cabinet files. Finally, he looks back at me. "Are you from here? Haven't seen you around?"

I lean back and sigh. "Sort of, I was... I just moved here from Kentucky. Well, I just bought the St Lindon's church and it would mean a great deal to me to gather some information about my mother." I pull out the newspaper clipping to prove that I was found at the St Lindon's church and show them my adoption records. He looks at the papers and looks up at me.

"So, you were the mystery baby that was found in 1962 at St. Lindon's? I remember back when the whole town had talked over it for years." He sits back into his chair.

"I know this is a lot to ask, and I was wondering if you had any articles about Mary's disappearance when they found her dead later in the lake?" He sits straight up in his chair this time and looks straight at me.

"Yes, let me look here." He looks at a small folder and flips through the pages. "I might have some articles to print out from the microfiche." "Hold on a second I will be right back." He gets up and shuts the door. I knew her name was Mary O' Conner from the newspapers but that was all I had. I sit and wait nervously hoping that he has found enough information. It is ten minutes before he comes back with a stack of copies in his hands.

"Okay, I found these articles we can copy for you." I had one more question to ask before I left. "Do you remember if there had been any witnesses about who was with her that night?" He looks through the papers. "I remember there was an older woman who had attended the St Lindon's Catholic church. She was questioned a few times about the girl, when she turned in a rosary, she said she had found it on the bridge. The girl had been staying with her when she was pregnant. No one knew it had been Mary's baby that was left at the church. Her and her son had been trying to help the girl but we thought she had runaway. It seemed suspicious because she was family and they wanted to get her to go to rehab. She just kept showing up missing until we found enough information to suspect that something wasn't right. She hadn't gotten on the train that she supposedly was going to take that day. They had turned in a train ticket she said she found in Mary's room, and a red sweater to help with the investigation. Sometimes I'm not sure what really happened myself."

"What was the woman's name who found the rosary?" I ask. The officer looks at the paper again. "The woman's name was Sarah Mason. Sarah passed away a while ago, but her son David Mason is a priest now at St Mary's down the street, he might have more answers to your questions then we do."

I take the articles and put them under my arm. "Thanks, so much for your help." I bite my lip and realize that Father David had been keeping this information from me. I wasn't ready to hear all this yet. "You know she was young and maybe her heart was broken. It's terrible when I have to witness these sad stories over tragedies like this. I am sorry." I nod as I stand up to leave.

"Do you have any information about the investigation of the church after the 1992 fire?"

He looks at me and then hesitates. "Well, we did have some investigators go over there afterwards, but I remember that they couldn't finish, they swore that they heard something down in the basement in Father Eugene's room. They didn't find anything unusual that kept causing the fire alarm to go off. The fire department was called on several times to find that there was no fire in the building. Mrs. Wilkinson, if you are worried about your safety, we can't help you. I am sorry. Maybe you should have it checked out by a professional. Likely, it's just a bunch of voodoo if you ask me. "I don't believe in ghosts myself."

I think about the noises I was hearing and what I had seen earlier in the basement. There was nothing that seemed threatening. "No, it's okay. I'm just having trouble adjusting I guess."

I turn on First St and look at the St Mary's Catholic church that I always passed on the way back. Father David was the priest there. I wasn't raised Catholic but since living in my church I had felt some connection to the beliefs. I look at the steeple rising high as if it's the only beacon of light waiting for those in town to come to it. It had replaced the St Lindon's long ago since it closed. I had wondered if I should start attending just to watch and investigate Father David. There was something suspicious and mystifying about him. It made me feel anxious but I didn't know why, maybe he was holding back something from me.

My imagination had always' saved me from seeing the black and white in situations, that's why I felt I had to find a realistic explanation for anything. Now I wished that I could take away all that insecurity I sometimes held onto. Maybe my real mother had felt the same way when she had to hide behind her lie. No one had known she was pregnant and she had to hide it from the town. If she was told that she wasn't ready to be a mother because of her problems, maybe she just felt alone and didn't want to seek the help that she should have. I wondered if she had felt like I did when I had wanted to look good under everyone else's standards when deep inside I was really struggling. It's not a comforting feeling when you must hide behind a lie, until someone sees you for who you really are.

I turn on Middletown Road and park my truck in my driveway. This strange town was all becoming real to me. I walk through my door and feed my cat Ramona. I sit down at my kitchen table and look at the papers in order that the officer gave me. I straighten my bifocals under the dim light. I pause when I see an article that dates back to August 5th, 1962:

Girl of Lindon Catholic Church Disappears.

"Father Eugene was questioned yesterday about a seventeen-year- old young girl that had been attending his church. On the night of August 5th Mary O' Conner was last seen coming from the St Lindon's church. One witness David Mason, told authorities that he had spoken with the girl over a train ticket but he did not know where she was going. Due to lack of information, our detectives on duty are trying our best to track down as much information as we can. We in the town of Waynesville are doing everything possible to find witnesses. The seventeen-year-old will be posted as missing until further evidence is found. Posters of Mary O' Conner's photograph will be put out at nearby community centers and public services. If anyone has any information, please contact the Waynesville police Department until further leads."

I continue skimming through the articles and find another paper dated August 12, 1962 that contains another article about her.

Missing Girl's Rosary Found Near Bridge
Where She Disappeared.

"Thirty-nine-year-old Sarah Mason turned in a rosary yesterday she had found on the bridge. She had told the police that it had belonged to seventeen-year-old Mary O' Conner. One witness has come forward so far, in telling the authorities that Mary had told her that she was going to meet someone at the train station that night. However, it appeared that she did not get on the train. The foster family whom she has been staying with has been questioned about her drug addiction. Due to lack of information, we are waiting to continue the search and questions until further information has cleared."

Then I find one more article. This one is dated August 28, 1962.

Missing Girls Body Recovered in Lake
Due to attempted Suicide.

"Mary O' Conner's body was found in Buckeye- lake under the bridge yesterday morning. Due to a red sweater and rosary that was turned in by a witness, the dogs picked up a scent identified to belong to the girl. The area under the bridge was inspected and a piece of hair was found in the dirt to be evidence. The investigation performed an autopsy and has found reason to believe that this was not an accident. The seventeen-year-old girl had sustained severe injuries from the impact including a broken neck. This criminal investigation has not identified if this was a suicide or homicide. Due to the questionable state of the body at the time of death, the injuries are being investigated for further details as to when this happened. The state of the body has shown that she had perished weeks before. We in the city of Waynesville will continue to question witnesses and anyone else who can come forward with more information."

I look at the black and white picture of the girl dressed in a white dress. She had looked so much like me at that age. She had the same piercing light eyes and dark wavy hair I had. I bite my lip, why was the sad story they all had kept from me? Why hadn't my adoptive parents told me the whole story? I knew they had been hiding something from me about it all those years. It's worse than a lie when someone keeps the whole truth from you. It's not fair when those who love you hold on so tightly that they protect you, not giving you room to feel the pain…

Chapter Twenty-Two
(David)

David looked out the window of his church office and watched as the cars passed by. He watched the pedestrians on the streets crossing the light, and the workers walking the streets during the lunch hour. Finally, it looked like some boys were coming from a baseball game. They passed the church and he could hear them making jokes about it behind his window. He didn't understand why some people didn't take religion seriously. It wasn't just about rules and confession but so many people had questioned him about it. He had tried to explain that Jesus was a relationship with the believer and that the church was a place where one learned how to become sanctified.

There had been some rumors over the years that David was gay. It wasn't true. Just because he couldn't marry and had to follow the rules didn't mean he wouldn't be tempted. It was his choice and his commitment to God to be a priest. Before he had become a priest, he had been in love. It was such a silly stereo type, that he started to ignore the way some looked at him. If he shook a male's hand, or put his hands over someone to pray sometimes it seemed awkward. It was just normal to feel wanted and sometimes he had to make sure he didn't overstep his boundaries. He had a reputation in town but he knew people could say hurtful things about him that weren't true. It was the price he paid for being known and respected by so many people.

The day of Mary's funeral had been so long ago but David remembered it as if it was just yesterday. He remembered holding onto his silver crucifix, as if he couldn't let go of something- else. He thought she had so much to live for. She had told him about her college plans to become a nurse. The moment he realized there was nothing he could do to take it all back, it had broken him. He and his mother had sat up front with the rest of Mary's family. Everyone knew that she hadn't many friends. But the town had questioned the girl's pregnancy. Where was the baby now? And who was the father? Some had pointed a finger at David. He watched them throw flowers, notes, and then the dirt on top of her grave until it was covered and hidden. His mother had stood next to him quietly looking down as if hiding under her black rimmed hat. David couldn't speak he had been at a loss for words too. He had still been in denial of it all.

From that day forward he kept punishing himself thinking of what he could have done differently. His mother had kept blaming him for getting Mary pregnant in the first place. David had wanted to become a priest and he couldn't pause his life and give up his commitment. Then the baby that was taken away always came back to haunt him. He had wondered what she had been like, her name, and even if she had looked more like him or Mary. The only thing that kept him moving on was hoping that she would want to come back someday to find answers. He didn't want to go back and face the family, knowing that he had been questioned about being involved with her that night. He was ashamed of how the gossip in town had accused him and his mother of Mary's death.

David straightened his black tie as he looked at himself in the mirror. He gazed at the clock; it was almost seven thirty pm. He didn't know why he kept questioning it and wondering about Patty. She had reminded him so much of himself. Now he would see her in town, they would see each other, and she wouldn't be a stranger anymore. She had come asking questions and he was saddened by what she would find out. Soon she was going to come to him asking for answers. He was sure of one thing, that he wasn't going to let it bother him anymore, it was time for him to step up and be the father he should be.

David parked his truck and looked at the St Mary's church. It was another Mass service. It was smaller than what St Lindon's had been. This had been his church for so long but he knew someday he would have to leave it to someone else. He wondered who would take his place after he stepped down. David walked back onto the sidewalk towards the back door. The parking lot was filling up and as he glanced behind him, he saw a police car parked across the street. It made him feel insecure when they came to his services. He hoped they weren't just coming to protect the area. He hoped they wanted to listen to his sermons.

It was a late service, after Father David had said the Lord's prayer, he did his quick message of "Faith." He read from Matthew 4:18 and explained how the two disciples Peter and Andrew who were fishermen were asked to follow Jesus. "Jesus has chosen you to be an agent of change wherever you go. He has called us to Believe, Stand, Serve and Follow." The communion wine was held out for those who wished to come up. "This is my blood so sins may be forgiven. Do this in remembrance of me." He took a deep breath and smiled as he shook hands by the back door.

"Excuse me Father, but when is your "Sacrament of Penance?" I just need to catch up, it's been a while since I really followed my confessions." David couldn't concentrate as he tried to answer the questions. "How are you holding up?" they kept asking him about his lung operation and health. He didn't tell anyone about his diagnosis yet. He wasn't ready to tell everyone he was dying. He watched as officer Lawrence, the town policeman, nodded his head and waved as he went out the door. David felt his face turn red as he breathed a sigh of relief. The building was finally empty and the parking lot was cleared.

It was after nine as he looked over at the mess of papers on his desk piled high. Most were opened letters from people in the congregation thanking him for helping them with their problems or questions. Some were complaints telling him that the donations should have gone to the homeless down the street instead of the mission fund. But he couldn't please everyone's demands. He learned to step back a long time ago when it had become too much.

It was an hour after he noticed it getting late and becoming darker outside. As he went to lock the doors behind him, David stepped back in shock and looked behind the back door. Someone had sprayed graffiti over the door. "You can't save them!" It stared back at him in bright red paint. He had not seen or heard anyone from the last hour. Who was doing this? It did not make any sense as to why they kept bothering him. Whoever it was had been trying to scare him again. Over the years some outsiders had tried to shut his church down wanting to use the land for something else.

It was a milder night outside with the late July moon coming to take away the last summer equinox. David looked up at the full yellow moon as he walked back to his truck. He looked across the dark street to see if anyone had been watching him. Even though it was warm outside, he felt the hair on his arms stand up. Who was it that kept bothering him? David felt lost at this point. He had hoped over the years the town would forget. He would have to pray for protection for himself. He would have to get the door repainted again. How could he let it go if they kept reminding him of what they couldn't forgive? There was a book on his shelf at home, it was a collection of poems by Edna St Vincent Millay. He had one spot bookmarked on its page for a reason. "O God, I cried give me new birth, and put me back upon the earth, upset the clouds gigantic gourd, and let the heavy rain downpour. In one big torrent set me free, washing my grave away from me…"

Chapter Twenty-Three
(Patty)

It had been a long night, I had tossed and turned and kept seeing the face of Mary O' Conner every time I closed my eyes. Why was my past so full of secrets and lies? What was everyone trying to protect me from? I didn't have any evidence yet to prove it but I had the feeling Father David knew her more than just a friend. I have decided to stop by the St Mary's church during confession so I could ask him some more questions. He seemed to be a nice man and I had enjoyed talking with him. If his mother had found Mary's rosary I wondered if he still had it.

The real reason I couldn't let go of this was because I still felt I needed to know why. I didn't know what it was like to have a drug addiction but why did she give up on living? Maybe she had thought those guilted bars she hid behind would keep her safe, but instead she had been suffocating. She was like an innocent bird waiting to be set free. She had hidden behind that cage where she thought she was safe. She wanted so badly to be free, to just fly away, and to not worry about her circumstances. But sometimes no matter what, if you don't see that the door is open to free yourself, you don't want to get out; sometimes you feel safer hiding behind that unlocked cage, because there is no belief as to what's on the other side. It's belief that gets us where we want to be. If only she had been stronger in believing in what she could not see.

The good thing was I felt I was finally getting somewhere. I was reminded by a Bible verse I had learned in church. 2 Corin 12:9-10; "My grace, loving kindness, and mercy is sufficient for you, for my power is made perfect in weakness. That is why I delight in hardships, insults, and weaknesses."

I remembered the day Phillip had asked me to marry him. It had been about nine months since we started dating. We had decided to take a camping trip for the weekend. I had not wanted to camp in a hot tent for two days. I remembered worrying about what we would eat or how far the walk to the bathroom would be.

That night when we were laying outside under the night sky and looking up at the stars we began to talk. I had explained to him pointing at the constellations that I had made up my own names to them. He just laughed as I gave him descriptions of "Pegasus's Lady" or "Hydra's Tail" "Then he turned to me and reached into his pocket. "Every constellation is not the same, they all have patterns, every -one has a different purpose" he had told me, "But you are the only constellation that guides my North star." I fell into his arms as I looked for the ring in the light of the moon. "I don't have a ring yet." He laughed. There's nothing in this lifetime that can prepare you for that kind of decision. Inside, I had been hopeful and I knew he loved me. I didn't need a ring to prove it or define what we had. On the other hand, you can't hold back loving someone just because you are afraid you might lose them. That was the hardest part for me to believe, that no darkness would ever take away my shining star.

I arrive at the library two miles from town and do my research. I look for the obituary about Luke and hope I can find it. I finally come to the article from 1992. It seems he died two days later at the hospital. He had been an organ donor to several recipients it mentions. I read the details in the micro fish:

"Luke Bolan died yesterday at Memorial hospital from complications due to a heart condition. The thirty-two-year-old man had died in a tragic fire at the St Lindon's Catholic church he had attended for eighteen years. He had gone inside to save Father Eugene the fifty-four-year-old priest whom later was found to be asleep in his office. While the man was inside the roof had caved in over them but neither did not make it out safely. One by stander had pulled them out and by the time the medics had arrived both were unconscious. Luke died of heart complications due to the burns two days later. He worked as an electrician for Ford Electric for ten years and helped his wife at Marcella's coffee shop on Parson's St. He is survived by his wife Marcella and his mother Elizabeth. The town will never forget the brave man who gave his life to save another."

I look at the date again in bold black letters on the top page it was the day he had died; April 11, 1992. It was the same day Phillip and I had been in the accident.

Chapter Twenty-Four
(David)

David looked at the clock, it was two in the afternoon on a Saturday. He had a strange hobby; he had always' liked to watch birds. He knew what every type of bird was including red crested black birds, blue jays', and golden finches. Living out in the woods, he would sit on his porch with his binoculars, and watch them for hours. He didn't know why he was so fascinated with them. Maybe it was because they had a way of seeing the world from high above the clouds. They could see everything from a different point of view, as if transferring into another parallel world. Birds could fly long distances for miles and somehow never got lost. The most amazing thing to him, was that they would fly so far just to be with their kin. Sometimes he felt like a bird wanting to do anything just to reconnect to its lost kin. He had his problems, but he just let it fester under him. He had learned that in order for a bird to fly it needed the right shape of wings, and the right pressure and angle to stay in the air. A bird could glide in the wind as it didn't fight against it. In the same way, if he just changed his direction, he knew he could get to the place in his life where he needed to be. He needed to stop fighting against the wind.

It was a Tuesday afternoon at St Mary's and David was about to leave his confessional box when he heard someone come in. Today, he had waited in the dark booth like he did every Tuesday afternoon. He didn't mind sitting alone in the darkness waiting to hear the confessions of penitents. His long legs had gotten in the way but he could sit awkwardly so they wouldn't cramp up. He had learned from his mother, that he had been a strange boy, because he worried about too many things. He remembered when she took his hand when he had gotten older, because he was still scared of the dark; "Don't be ashamed." She had said, "fear helps us know that we need someone greater than ourselves."

He had gone to the small church alter room in the hospital that day his mother had been diagnosed with cancer, he got down on his knees and he begged God to not take her away from him. "Please…" he had begged, "Please forgive her. Don't take away her faith…" The day of the funeral David felt as if God had taken her from him for a reason. He didn't know yet what his mother had done. She had kept it from him until she was sick and dying. However, he realized that he shouldn't have asked for God's help in fear but in faith.

He felt strange sometimes sitting inside the old church in the middle of the day alone like this. He would look around at the high ceiling, and become mesmerized by the lighted shadows hitting the large wooden cross hanging high above the alter. He thought about how he sometimes wanted to get closer to God, but he had felt more compressed every time. In the same way, the closer he felt to letting go, the farther away he felt from himself. However, he wanted to be free from what was keeping him prisoner to his own incertitude. He didn't want to run from God anymore. Consequently, he knew he needed to change.

"Can I help you?" It was nearly four and someone came in and sat in the confession box.

"Yes, Father I am here for confession." The female voice sounded familiar, he felt dizzy as he tried to focus his eyes to see behind the floral decorated black screen. "Father David?" she told him. "I have a confession to make."

"Bless you for your sin. What is it you want to confess?"

"I, well… I sometimes wonder if I really loved my husband. He had his life and I had mine. But when he died after the coma, I felt less anxious. Do you think I should have felt different?"

David started to stretch his long legs as he sat down. He could see that it was Patty in between the lattice confessional window.

"Well, how long were you married?"

"Eighteen years to Phillip."

"Well, that's a long time to stick with someone if you don't love them." He knew what it felt like to carry the burden of guilt." David sank as he listened.

"Yes, but have you ever felt that you screwed up so bad that you couldn't fix your mistake? How does one forgive themselves in circumstances like this?"

"You can't blame yourself for every failure you make. We all make mistakes sometimes. When you admit to it, you own it, but it doesn't mean that you should feel bad. What was the last thing you remember about your husband?"

"I saw him lying peacefully in that hospital bed as if he was ready to go, I felt he didn't need me anymore. Maybe that's why it hurts so much. Will God forgive me? Is it because I feel like I failed him? I mean I don't like to talk about it but I do know that he loved me. I just wanted him to know that I was sorry."

"Patty, only you can ask God for forgiveness and in time you will forgive yourself." "Maybe letting him go like you did, meant you really loved him more than you think." It was quiet. David swallowed hard and closed his eyes. "It sounds like your husband was a good man, I am sure he is in Heaven with God. You shouldn't let it bother you, there was nothing you could have done. It sounds like he saved many lives in return. There is a Bible verse you should remember, 2 Corin 5:17; "So if anyone is a new creature in Christ, what is old has passed away. Behold all things have been made new."

"Father, can I ask you something?" "Have you ever been in love?" she finally asked him.

David hesitated at the question wondering why she would ask such a thing to a priest. "Well yes, there was a girl who liked me during my younger days but I had wanted to follow the parish."

It was quiet before she spoke. "Would you have done anything to be with her even if it meant leaving your dreams behind?"

David grew anxious as he thought of an answer. "Yes, probably if she was serious and I was. But you can't always believe that you must save someone just to keep them. Just like when you wanted to keep your husband alive, but couldn't. I tried to save the girl I loved but couldn't. It's not up to us sometimes to determine their purpose." David bit his lip and continued. "Patty you must believe that God has greater plans for all of us, in every circumstance there is a new beginning. He makes sense out of everything inevitable. What happened was something that you had no control over. Maybe God will show you the reason for your suffering someday." There was a long pause until he heard a shuffle and then he saw the door slightly open.

The last words she had spoken made the hair on his neck stand up. "Father, it's not fair, is it? if we love someone than why isn't loving them enough?"

It was after Patty had left that he started to cry, not just little tears but he wept like a baby. It had been so hard burying his feelings when he had been in denial for so long. Sometimes David had thought in the back of his mind that they both had died that day. Mary had died unhappy and that had hurt him. But here was his daughter asking him for the advice about loss and how to move on when he struggled to face his own. Nothing could have prepared him for such a question. He knew deep inside that he had always loved them both that was why it had been so hard for him to forgive himself. He needed to redeem himself for not facing the fact.

David remembered when they had buried Mary's casket at the Caesar cemetery. He had run off to be alone in the woods that day after her funeral. He kept walking and walking until he had passed over a small creek that ran through the back woods. The trail ran about two miles down the path. He didn't want to remember what she had done. His eyes were fuzzy from crying. He knew he would carry the memory forever.

He remembered looking into the creek ahead but noticed that there was no current, something was keeping the water from moving. As he walked over and around it, he saw something lying in the water. When he crept closer, he realized that it was a train ticket. What was it doing in the creek? He had wondered if it was the same one that had been turned into the police. He tore it up angerly and watched it slowly float down back into the lake.

It had frightened him, but he had always' wondered; what happens to people that die who leave the world so suddenly? Do they immediately just go to Heaven? Or do they become stuck in some black hole, waiting to crossover to where they should be, until they realize that they sometimes can't because of some unresolved guilt or sin they are still holding onto. Do they stay in that dark place forever until they find redemption and forgiveness? Is it too late when one dies? His mother had asked him. He sometimes wondered if that was why life seemed so full of second chances.

For him he would always feel stuck between forgiveness and mercy. He didn't want to wait until it was too late for him. He would be getting sicker and he knew he had to come to peace with his absolution. What was he afraid of? He knew that black holes were the most powerful thing in the universe; exceeding the force of gravity and time, where nothing can escape it. It could destroy everything alive around it, swallowing up anything that overtakes its path, greater than the speed of light. There is no way out when there is nothing left but a black void of empty space…

ֽ9

Chapter Twenty-Five
(Patty)

I look at the beautiful pink Kalanchoe flowers I had picked up at the Waynesville floral shop. I have just arrived at the Caesar creek cemetery to look for the graves of my mother, Luke, and Father Eugene. I follow the map given to me and soon see a large headstone with Luke Bolon inscribed on the front. There looks like a verse or something written between and I kneel down so I can read it:

"Wherever a beautiful soul has been there is a trail of beautiful memories. Gone but never forgotten." It says. I lay the flowers on top. The flowers were already turning yellow on the edges and starting to droop. I stand and look down. His wife Marcella was buried next to him. I glance at the tombstone. There is a pink ribbon painted on the front side for breast cancer. I had hoped Luke wasn't alone anymore up there in Heaven with his best friend and his father. I hadn't seen his mother around but I had hoped to find out if she was living nearby.

Then I walk over to Mary's tombstone. It reads: "In loving memory, Mary O' Conner born 1945-1962. Faith, Hope, Love are the three eternities; to look up and not down, to look forward and not back, and to look outward and not inward." It was a verse from Reverend Edward Everett Hale. I kneel down and touch the smooth rock; it looks different than the rest. I take the rest of my flowers and lay them on top. As I pick up a flower I dropped in the grass, something catches my eye. There is something shiny about eight feet from my foot, as I kneel closer, it looks like a necklace. When I pick it up, I see that it is someone's rosary. I look at the shiny red beads and then the cross at the end. It looks old and tarnished so I turn it over to see if there are someone's initials. On the back is M.O. I cover my mouth in surprise and feel overjoyed. I am not sure as to where this has come from. I think what are the odds? Could this have belonged to her? Someone must have dropped it but who? A tear from my eyes falls onto my check as I try not to cry. It was a sign that she knew I was here. I carefully put it in my purse.

I walk over to the other side to find Father Eugene's large headstone with the Catholic cross on the front. The verse inscribed reads: John 11:25; "I am the Resurrection and Life. Whoever believes in me, even though he has died, he shall live."

There are some things that can happen to you that will make you feel insignificant, but that doesn't mean you won't survive. I knew what it was like to feel as if my mother's past owned me, but the reality was the more I learned about her, the easier it was to accept her and forgive. On the other hand, there are things we shouldn't hide about ourselves sometimes just because we can't bear to face our own weaknesses. Those things that keep us at bay will always weaken us until we realize they no longer claim us. It was time for me to stop blaming myself and become the strong person I was meant to be.

What I couldn't understand was why everyone kept telling me to move on. Why pretend as if that person doesn't matter anymore? It felt like I had to forget the most important people in my life. It didn't make it any easier when everyone else claims that time would heal and make it go away. But the reality is forgetting just makes it harder. I didn't want to forget those people who had become a part of my life. If anything, in a way,

I felt closer to them now that they were gone. The reality was those memories could only be taken away from me if I kept repressing them.

I couldn't believe what Father David had told me. It all was making sense of why I felt abandoned. My mother Mary had just wanted to keep me but she couldn't due to her problems. Maybe she felt like I had that no one understood her when everyone else had given up on her too. Now that I read the article's, I could put the missing pieces back together. It was sad that I hadn't come here sooner to find out the truth. When I thought about it, I had always' believed in second chances. Sometimes you might make the same mistake again, or sometimes you learn to change something so you become confident not to repeat it. Did Phillip give those sick people waiting for donated organs a second chance? I had hoped that it was the best decision I had ever made in my life. He hadn't really known that he saved me that day when I had almost given up. I wished all along that someone like that could have saved my mother.

It is past nine o clock and I am once again back in my church house and sitting in bed. As I look around me, and at Phillips urn sitting on my bedroom shelf I knew that it was my choice to stop blaming my circumstances. Nothing could take away those photographs of places we had gone and things we had done. No one could take away those childhood years I had spent with my childhood friend Luke and those happy times, and no one could take away my mother's desire for wanting to love something so bad that it broke her heart. The only thing I could do now was look at the positive equation that had come out above all this. I had to remember how it felt to feel happy and as time went on life would get easier.

I close my eyes and finally remember pieces after the crash. Phillip had looked so peaceful with his eyes closed, as if wherever he had gone, he hadn't known the pain. I remember how I felt the impact and how the other truck had slid onto its side farther down the road as it caught on fire. The smoke covered our windows and blocked my view from the firetrucks and ambulances. Our car had caught on fire and I couldn't pry open the door to get us out. I remembered yelling at Phillip to help me, but he had already passed out. They weren't coming for us and soon I couldn't breathe anymore as the smoke filled the car. But there was something I couldn't understand, there had been a bright light before I had passed out. I had thought it was over, but I wasn't in pain, something else had pushed me back as if wanting me to hold on. I wasn't ready to die yet.

I take a deep breath and try to exhale. Sometimes I wished that I could just start all over with no memory to dwell under. With no identity to call me by name. It should have been me, I kept thinking, it should have been me lying in that hospital bed, unknown to the world around me, dying to be set free...

When I saw my husband lying there on that bed in his coma, there was no way that I could prove to anyone that he had tried to speak to me. At that moment, it was if he had been trying to tell me that he didn't want to be tied to those machines anymore. I know I heard him as if he was right there. He wanted them to turn off the machines keeping him alive. I remember squeezing his hand to see if I could get a response. There's something intimate about holding someone's hand. It's different when there in a coma. You want to feel that there's someone inside trying to reach you. It's almost as if you want to feel that connection so bad that it's as if you imagined it. I would talk to him and ask him questions hoping somewhere he could hear me. Hours would pass and even though I wasn't sure if he was aware, I kept holding his hand. I kept squeezing it to let him know I was there. "Please wake up." I cried to him. When I thought I had felt him,

I almost jumped up for joy thinking he was responding but then the machines beeped. Had it just been my imagination?

I had looked over the papers where they asked me if I wanted to donate his organs. I knew he would have wanted it, but did I? It wasn't just knowing that his parts would become a part of someone else, but it was knowing that a part of him wouldn't be whole anymore. I didn't understand why he had to be torn apart from me like this. "Please, God what do I do?" The voices of the singing angels that I heard behind us were so loud and clear; as if they were singing just for us. In that moment I didn't question why, but I questioned myself, was I ready to let him go so he could help those other life's still waiting to live? I knew that whatever I did it would be okay, because he had taught me that life always gives us another chance…

Chapter Twenty-Six
(Patty)

Soon enough someone is ringing my doorbell. I look up. "Hello Mrs. Wilkinson, I am detective Lawrence and this is officer Dennis."

I look at the tall man again and the heavy-set man who looks older than the other. "Come in." I politely offer some sweet tea as they sit down. Officer Lawrence sits down and looks at me with a serious glance. "This church really looks good now that it's being taken care of finally."

"Yes," I tell them. "I am glad I haven't had to many problems with it yet. Just some repairs and the strange noises coming from the basement."

"So, Patty what did you want to show us?"

"Yesterday I went to the Caesar Creek cemetery to visit my mother Mary's grave but I found this in the grass nearby it. Do you think it was hers?" I take out the envelope and carefully hand it to them. I watch Officer Dennis handle the rosary.

"Well, this does look older for this generation. I think they had retrieved a similar rosary back then according to the newspaper articles but then they must have given it back to a friend of the family."

"But don't you think it's strange that it has M.O. engraved on the back and it was at the cemetery by her grave when I was there?" I mention as he carefully handles it.

"Well, someone must have dropped it recently. All I can think of is if she had someone who had known her who had been visiting the grave."

"Oh, do you know if she had been close to Father David? I had spoken with him recently and he had told me they had been friends."

Officer Dennis looks at me awkwardly. "Well, there has been a lot of talk in town over the years what people suspected. But I heard that his mother had lied to the authorities about the night Mary had disappeared."

"Like what did she say?" I ask them.

"Well, she said she had found the rosary on the bridge but her son told us later that Mary had come to him about going to the train station. The time frames didn't add up. We had no evidence to question her more but some suspected they both were hiding information."

"Maybe you should talk to Father David, he had been a witness that night she had disappeared. He is at the St Mary's church down the road." Officer Lawrence tells me.

This time I was convinced that I needed to talk to this man again. "Another reason I asked you to meet me was because I was concerned about these strange noises I keep hearing down in my basement, it's coming from that boarded up room down there. I'm not sure if anything is serious, but can you unlock it so we can check it out?"

"Sure, but what do you think is down there?" he asks. They both look at me as if I'm nuts.

"I just want to see if it's the pipes that need fixed or just to clean it out." I explain.

We are finally down in my basement with the dim light from the ceiling. Officer Lawrence comes over to me, and seems nervous, as he looks over towards officer Dennis on the far side. "Well, I'm not allowed to say why, but I heard that when the other men had been in here eighteen years ago, they had to leave suddenly." Officer Lawrence looked at me as his eyes grew wide. His voice got lower as he whispered, "I heard they had to suddenly run out. Something down here scared them; something weird had come out from behind those walls."

"Oh." I respond. He points towards the room. "See" I tell him, I'm not hearing things." I walk look over to watch Dennis get his lockpick out. Finally, it comes lose and falls off. I watch as he pushes the door open. Suddenly there is a cloud of black ash dust coming out from the room. We close our eyes as it floats around us and disintegrates to the ground.

"Must have been from the fire." He exclaims. I let them go inside first as I follow.

I look around at the old wooden desk and podium that still has old communion cups stacked up and bowls underneath. I notice an old fireplace towards the back and walk towards it. It looked like the older kinds with the black iron gate in the front with its diamond shaped patterns. The officer's step over the ash dust on the floor and watch as I open the drawers of the old desk in front and look around. "This must have belonged to someone." Officer Dennis exclaims. I look at a strange red sweater he is holding. I suddenly feel queasy. It looked like the same one my mother had wrapped around me as a baby.

"How did that get in here?" I ask. "Is it yours?" Officer Monroe asks. "I had been wrapped up in that same sweater when I was left at the church. But I don't understand? Why is it here?" I try to think and remember. Had someone tried to hide it in Father Eugene's office? Why wasn't it destroyed in the fire?

"Patty are you okay?" Dennis comes over to catch me as I sit in the kitchen chair back upstairs. "I'm just feeling dehydrated I guess." I get up and pour myself a glass of iced tea; my head is throbbing as I try to figure out this mystery.

"Patty?" I jumped as the officers call my name from downstairs. "Well, we looked in that room for you but you might want to get those old pipes and that fireplace looked at maybe that's the problem. We did not see anything strange down there and we have no reason to look for anything that had broken through the fireplace. There is no way someone would have gotten inside with the door being locked. Are you sure the noise was coming from down there?" I nod but don't tell them what I saw earlier.

I sit in the chair after they leave. I stare at the wall in confusion and listen to the tick tock of the clock above my kitchen. Tomorrow I would go back to the library and search for the articles about the fire. I could not find anything else that would explain this. Maybe I was just forgetting things. I wanted to go back down there; something had drawn me towards that room as if there was something about it that I should remember. Why did I see an angel come from that room? I knew it was trying to help me with my grief but what was it trying to tell me?

I look for Ramona my new calico cat I had just gotten days before I had moved here. She still was shy and would hide from me under my bed. However, as I look underneath, she is not there. I try to call her name but she doesn't come. Thinking she is just asleep somewhere I get up to turn off my light. She had never disappeared before at night; she usually would come lie somewhere in my bed room. It was nearly midnight and I was too tired to worry about anything else.

In my dream I am in a church, the smell of smoke is everywhere. There is a bright light and I hear fire trucks in the background. Someone is shouting my name. I am suddenly terrified because I can't hear myself speak. I am spinning towards a tunnel, something is trying to guide me towards it, but I feel as if I have left something important behind. I look down and see my body lying in a casket. "Wait!" I cry. There are people surrounding me. Something is wrong, I can't talk. I am confused and can't breathe. Why doesn't anyone hear me?" I think. "Patty, you must live for me, please go back." I hear the voice ever so distant but familiar. I suddenly wake up.

It is past ten am and I realize I had slept later then intended. I check a second message from my phone Father David had left me a message wanting me to come to the church to meet him. He had something important to tell me. I had hoped he was going to tell me more about my mother.

I get up and walk to the kitchen. I look around, but I still cannot find Ramona who is usually sitting by my bed or in the kitchen by her food dish. "Here kitty, kitty?" I call as I search around but she does not come. It is then that I realize that the fireplace vent was left open. I get a bad feeling in the pit of my stomach. "Ramona?" I didn't think, there was anything down there she could get into.

"Kitty?" I call again. I bring her treats hoping she is just scared and just hiding somewhere. I thought I had closed the door last night, but my memory was getting bad. Ten minutes had passed and there is no evidence of her anywhere. I walk back down into the dark basement, bringing my flashlight and searching. She never liked being that far away from me however she also had never seen stairs before.

I don't know what had happened but I soon see evidence that she is lying motionless inside the office fireplace. The door was left open because I had planned on cleaning up the mess. I walk over and see the fuzzy top of her head sitting stiff. She didn't hear me. I kneel down and reach out to pick up her stiff body. She was cold. I wondered if she had maybe eaten some kind of mouse repellent that had been left inside years ago. As I pick up her dead corpse, I see no evidence of what has caused her to die, she had only been one year old. I curse to myself as I realize that it had been my fault, I should have made sure the door was closed.

Chapter Twenty-Seven
(Patty)

I couldn't help but think about what if things had been different? What if I was still with Phillip and we were still at our old house living in Providence would I have decided to come back here? Would I have wanted to look for answers about my mother? Losing those two people in my life had driven me to a different point. I no longer wanted to just look at that threshold; I wanted to cross over and face the other side. I had wanted her to become real to me as if she was the only thing I had left. It was something my father had told me. "When life changes there are two kinds of people, those chasing a moment and those being chased." Was I letting it chase me all this time and now that I had faced it, was I ready to move on?

Why did I always feel that my whole life, nothing stayed normal? Yet somewhere between then and now, I thought the death of my husband had changed me. Maybe my expectations were too high, in a world full of vanity. All I could do right now was hope that this church I now lived in would not haunt me. Was it because I still couldn't let go of the ghost from my past? This church held so many secrets of its own past, that somehow it held a part of me too.

I didn't want Phillip to die the way he had, it's not fair, is it? When the ones we love are taken from us so suddenly without question. How come it makes us so angry? Where are the people who are supposed to love us when we need them the most? I thought of my mother whom I never knew and how I had denied the fact that I didn't get to really know who she was. All those years I had the choice to search. I could have come back here sooner. I kept putting it off until later, until later became never. Who you come from shouldn't be questioned, yet in the end all you have is the truth, no matter how painful it is you have to embrace what you are a part of. The good, the bad, and all the stuff that makes us human; we need to stop hiding from what's there. Sometimes' it's the only evidence that can save you.

The ghost like memory rose up before my eyes. I think about a memory from when I was seven and Luke was about ten. It was late summer and we were playing in his garage because it had been raining outside. In the corner of the door, I had found a small chrysalis hanging from a ladder up against the wall. I looked at it and wondered if it had an insect inside. "Luke, come and look at this!" I had told him. He came over and looked at the shell. He had wanted to open it, to see what was inside. "No!" I cried, "we have to wait until it turns into a butterfly, it must come out on its own." I explained to him.

"But what if it doesn't come out?" he had asked me. I tried to explain to him that it would die, if we ruined its protective shell too soon. We had to let it come out on its own. So, as weeks passed, we would look at that cocoon and wait. I had to keep telling him to not touch it, and to leave it alone. It will take time I told him, because it needs to gain its strength.

I had hoped to understand that one doesn't need to see something in order to believe it is there. Likewise, there was something alive and changing inside that cocoon, but we didn't need to see it in order to know that something was in there. I felt the squishy cocoon one day, and the thought haunted me; what if it had died? Maybe we had handled it too much, or maybe it had decided to just stay inside it's comforting shell. Seeking warmth and sleepiness the chrysalis had grown used to the darkness, taking away its strength to get out to survive. I had wanted to understand it, and to believe in what it could become, as it would fight its way out and open its new wings. But instead, we were left with nothing but dismay.

Months passed as it hung there, unchanged. Under its vulnerability the caterpillar had died. It hadn't been strong enough I told Luke, as we cradled the cocoon and buried it in his backyard. It hadn't wanted to come out because it was trapped fighting under its sad layer of worthlessness. Maybe it didn't want to fight over the outside world that might overtake it. It had died because it didn't believe that there was this beautiful place outside its shell, that would have given it a chance to use its new wings. If only it had just happened, I had thought, why couldn't it believe? Luke laughed at me as I cried over some dead insect. I thought of my real mother and how she had given up. "Why does a denied expectation hurt more than a denied hope?" I had asked my mother.

There was a butterfly somewhere starting to emerge under this chrysalis. I had wanted to accept those terrible things that happens when we sometimes expect too much. When it came to religion and believing in God, I had wanted to trust that there was something else greater outside of that cocoon hidden underneath my world. There are no equations, theories, or scientific rules that stand alone, to prove that we must separate ourselves, from the core being of where we have come from. One doesn't need scientific proof that there will always be someone else who predetermines everything that happens next. The truth is, something created that complex butterfly giving it a journey of its own. In order for that insect to even change from a caterpillar, it has to fall apart, it must surrender to the darkness around it, and decompose down to nothing but liquid. It must transform before it can be put back together again. It must survive the rebirth of being broken apart. However, if it cannot make that journey on its own it will die. This was a lesson about metamorphosis for us all; that if we don't surrender to whatever can consume us, then we will never be able to embrace that ambient light waiting for us on the other side outside our universe. It was time I faced the truth; I didn't like being ripped apart from what I had held so close. In the same way, I was suffocating under my own hopelessness wondering what lay ahead for me. I couldn't break free from what I had gotten used to. I couldn't see that on the other side there were others like me going through the same grief. Nevertheless, sometimes surrendering to our circumstances is the only way to survive.

Chapter Twenty-Eight
(David)

The letter from the hospital still lay on his kitchen table it was piled under his medical bills and ads. David sat down and looked at it. Did he really want to know? What did it matter anyways? I don't need to write a thank you letter to the hospital he thought. I just wanted the name of the doner. They had told him the recipient at the hospital but he couldn't remember. He did feel much better since the operation but the cancer had spread and not even chemo was an option. He took the envelope and slowly opened it. He pulled out the small piece of paper. "Date: May 2011: Doner: Phillip Wilkinson. Organ: right lung." He knocked over his glass of water catching the glass before it fell to the floor. David stood up in disbelief. He felt like this all had just been a dream. This can't be true he thought. The doner had been Patty's husband.

David looked at the clock above him. He didn't want to hide behind his mask anymore. He had called Patty later and she had met him in his office. He had wanted to tell her the strange news. He remembered how shocked she was when he told her that he had her husband's lung. "It's God's way of telling us that he's still here with you. See we were meant to experience this miracle." He told her. Patty had tears of joy as she listened to him tell her about Mary her mother.

Patty stared wide eyed at him as he told her how he had been so heartbroken over hearing that Mary had been found in the lake due to suicide after he had tried to reason with her. Then how he later found out that his mother was to blame all along.

"Sarah my mother had killed her, it was a hit and run. She couldn't confess because she felt guilty, but she lied to me and the authorities. Mary didn't die of a suicide like they had thought, it was an accident." He told her how the autopsy had discovered A contusion on her pelvic bone, questioning the fall from the bridge. "The police had some evidence but not enough to prove. Some people in town had suspected that we were lying about where she went that night." He told her. "I should not have gotten involved with someone like her. They kept pointing a finger at me after I became a priest, as if I wasn't good enough to help those turn from their own sins. It had weakened my faith as I struggled under the suspicions. It took me some time to forgive my mother for lying but I still struggle with it. I know it is in God's hands now.

He had been angry at himself for not getting the courage to look for Patty. I knew you were with your adoptive family so I thought you were fine without me. I was afraid they had already told you the details. The reality was, I couldn't forgive my mother, and I couldn't forgive myself for not being a better person and father. I shouldn't have been so insecure and selfish he admitted. Patty seemed at peace now that she knew that her mother hadn't really wanted to abandon her but wasn't able to keep her because of the drug addiction. "I feel like I hate you but I can't because you are my real father. This time I think we saved each other, but it's hard to forgive someone else when you can't forgive yourself isn't it?" She asked him.

He looked over at her seriously and nodded. She hadn't pitied him after all.

"I hope this won't change us because there hasn't been a day that goes by that I hadn't thought of you. Will you please forgive me? I need someone like you right now in my life."

Patty looked at him and paused. "I will pray for us and I forgive you for getting involved in this. I'm so sorry that things couldn't have been different. Would you like to come to my birthday candlelight eulogy?" she asked him. "It would mean a lot to me." It was a candlelight service for the whole town to remember those that died in the church fire and for those she had lost. Most people in the town had not realized that Patty had been Mary O' Conner's daughter. "Just like you I'm tired of secrets." She had told him.

Before she left David took her hand. "I'm dying. The cancer has spread. I could have some time but not long. The new lung wasn't enough. I hope we can take advantage of the little time we have left." he explained to her.

David thought of the hope he had carried for his daughter, she had lost her husband and best friend, now he was all she had left. He used to think this was all just a nightmare that he kept telling himself as if it never would end. He kept believing the lies that he told himself when he thought he wasn't good enough to be a father. It was why he had been so angry. However, it was never supposed to be that way. He had just let it become the threshold that had held him back. The good thing was Patty hadn't been remorseful. She understood that he didn't want to remember or tell her about the terrible accident. He had loved Mary and his heart had been broken. She knew what that was like as she was grieving over her husband. He should have trusted that she would have forgiven him. Was that why he felt so far away from happiness? He could not surrender to the forgiveness that he knew was waiting for him. He believed that it was the cancer that made him rethink about regrets in his life. Now it seemed this was God's way of giving him a second chance to step up, even though he wished he had more time. "You have brought me back to where I should be." He told Patty.

"God always gives us another chance." Patty told him. They hugged and she promised to be there for him at the hospital. "I'm proud of the father you have become." She cried. 'Mary had always loved you more than anything, and I think that's why she couldn't let you go.' He told her.

"Please take this, I want you to have it. I found it by Mary's grave." Patty took out a small rosary from her purse. She laid it in David's hands. He looked down at it, he knew it would come back to him somehow.

David sat back in his desk chair and looked over at the boxes he had packed up. He looked up at the calendar he took off his office wall. He always marked August 3rd as a special day year after year. He wanted to always remember the girl he had loved and the baby he had left behind. Tomorrow was her birthday; it would be different than the rest; they had finally found each other.

David no longer felt the darkness of his past consuming him and he hadn't expected so much to happen over the past month. He looked at the rest of the empty boxes on the floor and started packing. He was resigning from the parish because he would have to stay in the hospital. God had brought him back to his daughter and she was just the way he had always imagined her to be. He looked at the Bible verse on the paper weight on his desk. It stared at him as if it was meant just for him. "But you are a chosen generation, a royal priesthood, so that you may announce the virtues of him who called you out of darkness into his marvelous light." 1 Peter 2:9. He felt he was finally at peace and ready to die whenever that would be.

David took a deep breath. "God..." he prayed. "I need conviction for not trusting in your faithfulness. I hurt a lot of people I had loved and need final absolution. Forgive me for not trusting in your holiness, I know that my salvation is not earned through works, but by growing through you and learning to face my weaknesses. I know that you have given me this opportunity to come back to you. Help me get through this struggle in my life, as I rely on you daily until we meet again." Somewhere in the outside sanctuary he could hear a choir singing. "Hallelujah, Hallelujah." He would miss listening to the organ and the loud pipes as it echoed throughout the building.

It wasn't a religious song but David had remembered it was Mary's favorite.

He listened to the verses of the song; "And even though it all went wrong; I'll stand right before the Lord of song. With nothing, nothing on my tongue but Hallelujah..."

David looked at the painting of Jacobs latter one final time that hung on his wall above his desk. He knew that telling his daughter what had happened helped him move on. She had forgiven him and that's what he needed to hear. He wanted to reassure her that she wasn't forgotten just because her mother had died the way she had. Likewise, Mary no longer was an invisible ghost in her mind. Consequently, he wanted her to realize that he had always loved her and that she was never meant to be abandoned. He hoped that Mary was smiling down at him from Heaven and waiting for him to return. What was it about superhero's he had read about? "Our greatest glory is not in never falling but in rising every time we fall."

Chapter Twenty-Nine
(Patty)

Today, August 3rd was my fiftieth birthday, we were going to have a ceremony outside of my house at nine pm to light candles. No one had questioned me as to why I had bought the St Lindon's church, or why I had wanted to own someplace with such a dark past. I had put the red sweater on the one we had found in the office basement. I hadn't known how it got into father Eugene's office but I didn't question it. The only explanation I could think of was that someone had put it there after my mother was found. I quickly grab the Chinese sky lanterns' that I collect from a box. It was only seven o'clock, but I wanted to be prepared for what we were going to do. I was going to give each person one so they could remember their loved ones and we were going to let them go. Even though they had a small flame inside they were perfectly safe floating in the sky.

When it's finally time, the small crowd gathered at my front lawn has grown larger. I had hung special Christmas lights around the church house for the ceremony. You could probably see them for miles lighted up from down the road. About twenty people had shown up. I quickly hand out the lighted sky lanterns.' I see that officers Lawrence and Dennis were standing in the back. I look around at the people gathered so quietly in my front lawn. Some had even asked me if I had experienced any strange hauntings yet. I thought about it, but I didn't want to tell anyone what I had thought. I was sure that it hadn't been my imagination. I hoped I could now believe in angels, even if I did not understand what I had experienced, at least it had given me something to believe in.

We wait a couple of minutes for more people to show up. Soon I see another truck pull onto the street. It was Father David. I wasn't sure what to expect but I had hoped he would show up. It was a small town but no one else knew that I was his daughter yet. However, I had his permission to tell everyone that he had Phillips's lung. I also wasn't going to reveal the information David had told me about his mother with Mary's death. Knowing the truth was enough for myself. I wave as he grabs a lantern and joins the crowd in the back. An old woman slowly comes my way leaning on a cane, she looks to be in her eighties. "Miss Davidson? I am so sorry; for your loss. Do you remember me? I was Luke's mother." I stare at the woman standing beside me. "It is so great to finally see you again." I hug her as she takes a candle, "but it's Mrs. Wilkinson." I whisper to her.

I face the crowd before me. "Well, I guess I would first like to say thank you all for coming, this means a lot to me. I will just give a couple words about myself. My name is Patty Wilkinson and I was left as a baby by Mary O' Conner in 1962 fifty years ago from today at this church. I wanted everyone in this town to get the story right that she didn't give me away on purpose. Even though rumors say that she was troubled and on drugs that didn't mean she was a bad person. Mary had struggled like we all do but that doesn't mean she was weak. You all might not have remembered the story, but her body was found in the lake a couple weeks after I was born. She had trouble stopping her drug addiction but couldn't find a way to move on. It grieved me that she hadn't wanted to change causing those around her to struggle too. The truth is not always what it seems sometimes when we don't have all the evidence. You might not believe it was true, but I am glad she did have people in her life who had loved her and tried to direct her towards the right path."

"I had always believed it didn't matter who or where I came from but coming here and digging up answers to my past made me realize that we are always looking for hope. The truth is she died a Hero even though she couldn't face the demons that took her down. I am grateful to the officers of this town and for those who helped me face this closure in my life. Mary will be remembered for the young woman, friend, and daughter that she once was."

"Luke was my best friend from childhood who died in the church fire of 1992 that had happened here not too long ago. He will also be remembered as the person who taught me that the best kinds of people are the ones who unexpectedly come waltzing into your life. This church carries a past with a history of tragedies but good memories that won't be forgotten. We in this town shouldn't forget the priest Father Eugene whom had made this place a safe haven for those seeking answers to their faith. We also should thank Father David who had tried to save them from the fire."

"Please take your lantern and think about who you want to remember. The lantern you have in your hand is symbolic of letting go of our grief and beginning a new path, the light inside stands for rebirth and what will illuminate our future." When everyone was ready, I motion for them to let go of their string. I watch as I see David standing in the back with his. I take mine and watch everyone's lantern float high above the trees into the now darkened sky. I continue.

"When I was a little girl, I had always wanted to skip to the end of a story that my mother had read to me. I didn't like wondering what was going to happen next. I didn't understand that sometimes we have to get through the middle of the story before we can understand the end." I wipe a tear that slowly falls from my cheek. "It was a terrible thing that had happened to my husband. He recently died in an accident. However, he had donated his organs and now standing before you Father David has received his lung. It's funny how life can come back to you, to remind us that sometimes tragedies are a miracle in disguise. There is a saying my husband used to say; 'Tomorrow will be better than yesterday because Hope begins with another chance.'

I yelled out the last eulogy: "The great Christopher Columbus might not have been the first one to discover that the earth was round, but he opened a way for us to realize that perhaps God made the earth more circular so we would not see too far down the road. Our destination never ends up looking the way we expect. We can never plan our destiny, when there will always be something else redirecting our future. However, it's belief that gets us to where we want to be, it helps us see what we need to believe in."

Everyone sang happy birthday to me as I smiled at David far across the crowd. My wish had already come true. I had found what I had come looking for already. My story of finding out my past wasn't ending it was just beginning. I had a father who had loved me and was waiting for me to accept his love. Was this our chance to begin a new friendship but end with sadness and peace? Sometimes we don't realize how much God is hurting waiting for us to come back and acknowledge his forgiveness. Life is full of mercy and compassion all around us because God wants us to learn how to forgive. Can we also learn from the past and forge ahead, so we can learn from our mistakes?

After everything I had been through, I had survived despite the long dark tunnel I had been stuck in. That time when I lost my husband, I didn't look back with guilt, instead I knew I had to stop blaming myself and face the in between of my life where I still felt stuck. When I realized, those I had loved were physically gone, I knew that they would always stay in my heart.

My parents, my mother, my husband, and my best friend would always be the family I never had.

I had been that vulnerable child, living next door to a stranger, not knowing that he would become my best friend, and someday a hero. I had been that little girl, with wishes and dreams of finding my real mother, only to find out that she couldn't live without me. And I had been that woman depending on the man of my dreams to save me, not knowing that suddenly he would be taken; to only show me how to embrace life as it is. Now that I had lived through it all, and had faced those circumstances despite the fact; that blank page in my life had so many new stories yet to tell. I had come out on the other side stronger than ever before, not just because I had survived, but because I didn't look back with regret or sorrow. Instead, day by day, I was still learning to find peace in my heart.

I was reminded of something Luke had promised me one time. "You and I will always be besties. We will always find a way to connect with each other because friends never forget." I had always believed it, and I had held onto that promise, because someday if not in this life, I knew that friendships never die. I stared at the flickering lanterns now far off into the distance. It wouldn't be long until the flames would disappear and they would fall to the ground. It seemed so easy to just let go and follow the easiest but longest journey towards that horizon I had denied for so long. Somewhere in the far distance before me I see them fading away. Luke was smiling at me where he is his young self again. My husband Phillip also was standing in the distance, and next to them was my mother Mary smiling over at me as if she is proud. Behind them were my adoptive parents standing as if waiting for me. I knew they were on the other side somewhere; but it wasn't my time yet. God had plans for me here on Earth, where there were so many things, I still needed to do. Now I knew what it meant to be truly loved.

I look up at the millions of stars above me and think of how God has always planned it. Some stars burn the brightest right before they die, but it can take hundreds of years or more before it reaches earth. When looking at the universe we are looking back at time itself. Somewhere in my peripheral view, I knew that my lantern wasn't ready to fall to the ground yet but I could see it sinking.

They say our memories will live on if we keep them close to our heart. But we live our life and ask ourselves what do we leave behind after we die that will last? What is the value of a memory? Can what we believe be the same as what we hold in our heart? Love it is the common denominator of all we have left. We must hold onto it, let it shine in us, and wrap its arms around us. It's all we need to finally guide us home...

Chapter Thirty
(Louisville Hospital)

"**P**atty, can you hear me? Patty?" I open my eyes but I don't know where I am or what has happened. There is a tube stuck down my throat and I can't talk. I look over at the doctor standing by my bedside. "Her name tag says, "Dr. Angel Hernandez." "Patty, please open your eyes." I look around the room and see that I am in a hospital bed connected to machines. "You are in a hospital. You were in a bad car accident two days ago. I'm sorry, but the other man who was with you died. Do you remember what happened?" I look at my hand missing it's wedding ring. I look at the calendar nearby on the wall and it says April 1992 instead of 2011. I am confused as to what is going on. I jump up, shake my head, and try to speak. "We had to do major surgery because you injured your liver. You flatlined. We almost lost you, your heart stopped for three minutes, but we revived you. You needed a liver transplant, and luckily, we found a match for your negative type AB. You are a very lucky woman." I nod my head in confusion. She hands me a white board and a marker. I write on it hoping for an answer and show it to her. Just a moment, let me find out I will be back soon. When she comes back in, she shuts the door behind her. "The thirty-two-year-old man from Waynesville, Ohio who donated his liver to you, his name was Luke Bolan."

Epilogue

Faith Hope and Love are the three eternities; to look up and not down, to look forward and not back, and to look outward and not in.

–Reverend Edward Everette Hale.

Acknowledgments

This book is dedicated to anyone who has lost someone important in their life, whether it be a child, family member, brother, sister, husband, wife, or friend. Thanks to all those who helped me edit and revise this book. Thanks to my best childhood friend, who gave me the best childhood memories of growing up in the eighties. Thanks to my parents for helping me to never give up on my dreams. Thanks to my husband my earth angel, for putting up with my hours away at the computer writing, and for giving me the advice I needed. A special thanks to my whining cats for being patient and letting me work instead of playing with them. And finally, thanks to my eighty-three- year- old friend Jeanette, who had lost her husband and son to a drunk driver, and taught me that forgiveness can heal the heart. Even if you can't find the light be the light.

This work is fiction and is not meant to disparage any particular religion or beliefs.

People are like stained glass windows they sparkle when the sun is out; but when the darkness sets in their beauty is revealed only if there is a light from within. -Elizabeth Ross

CPSIA information can be obtained
at www.ICGtesting.com
Printed in the USA
LVHW032337041221
705313LV00007B/391